Coming Home to You

Coming Home to You

An Orchard Hill Romance

Rebecca Crowley

Coming Home to You
Copyright© 2022 Rebecca Crowley
Tule Publishing First Printing, September 2022

The Tule Publishing, Inc.

ALL RIGHTS RESERVED

First Publication by Tule Publishing 2022

Cover design by Erin Dameron-Hill

No part of this book may be used or reproduced in any manner whatsoever without written permission except in the case of brief quotations embodied in critical articles and reviews.

This is a work of fiction. Names, characters, places, and incidents are products of the author's imagination or are used fictitiously. Any resemblance to actual events, locales, organizations, or persons, living or dead, is entirely coincidental.

ISBN: 978-1-957748-93-1

Chapter One

"Flush-mount hanger. Self-drilling hanger. D-ring hanger. Bear-claw hanger. Sawtooth hanger. Hanging *system*."

Mabel Antonoff propped her hands on her hips, gazing up at the towering array of hooks and wires, and sighed.

Why did hanging a picture have to be so complicated?

The heavy, thudding sound of several sets of steel-toed boots racing toward her jerked her out of her picture-hanging mind spiral, and she glanced up just in time to see two store employees racing past.

"Call 911," one of them barked breathlessly into his walkie-talkie. "We have a medical emergency in aisle twelve."

Mabel didn't waste a second. She dropped the array of hanging apparatuses she'd compiled and took off running.

She'd barely gone three steps when the rearmost employee turned to her with his hands up. "Ma'am, there's no need to be alarmed, but I need to ask you to—"

"It's okay, I'm a nurse."

He looked doubtful, and she sighed inwardly. She was, in fact, a master's-qualified advanced practice nurse, a certified nurse-midwife, and a credentialed surgical first assistant, but she frequently came up against the assumption that her job title meant she spent her days drawing blood and fluffing pillows.

She was on the brink of informing him that she knew just as much as the paramedics who'd be on their way when she heard a distinctly solid, belly-rooted moan that could only mean one thing.

Someone was giving birth.

She darted around the employee, who thankfully gave up on his effort to delay her and followed instead. She sprinted through the aisles, pausing only long enough to read the numbers, before taking a hard right at aisle twelve—plumbing and bathroom fixtures.

Mabel elbowed her way through a pack of well-intentioned onlookers to find three men crouched around a heavily pregnant woman sitting on the floor: a bewildered-looking store manager, according to his shirt; a semihysterical man wringing his hands who she suspected was the soon-to-be father; and a broad-shouldered man whose authoritative posture suggested he'd stepped in to get the situation under control.

Mabel ignored everyone except the expectant mother. She knelt beside the woman and took her hand, smiling warmly.

"Hey, hon. I'm Mabel, and I'm a midwife. What's your name?"

"Ashley," she said through clenched teeth.

"How far along are you, Ashley?"

"Forty weeks and three days. My husband thought walking around the hardware store might help bring on labor." Ashley shot the hand-wringing man a lethal glare.

Mabel relaxed slightly. The baby was full-term—and in a hurry, as evidenced by Ashley's long, gut-deep moan as another contraction overtook her.

She glanced up at the manager, who stood behind Ashley. "Can we get some clean towels or blankets? Maybe a couple of pillows?"

The manager nodded briskly and bolted down the aisle, shoes squeaking on the linoleum floor.

In her peripheral vision Mabel sensed the third man—the take-charge one—rise to his feet and start to back away.

"Not so fast," she addressed him, not taking her eyes off Ashley's face as she beckoned him back with her free hand. "Can you get everyone out of here and set up some kind of perimeter? We can't block the route for the paramedics when they arrive but maybe you could find—"

"Mabel, it's me."

She didn't recognize the voice. Oh God, was it someone she'd dated? Coaching herself to be polite despite her growing exasperation, she glanced over her shoulder.

Suddenly it all made sense: this was a dream. There was no other possible explanation for the presence of Sam Strauss, the man she'd once believed was the love of her life and whom she hadn't seen in over a decade, here in this hardware store in Orchard Hill, Missouri.

But if this was a dream, shouldn't he look younger? Closer to the teenage version she'd known? Not that this Sam hadn't improved with age. In fact he looked better at thirty than he had at eighteen. His shoulders had broadened and his cognac-brown hair remained thick and full. He wore well-cut jeans, an unremarkably gray long-sleeve shirt, and paint-splattered sneakers. His stormy-sea eyes were sharper and wiser, yet the faint creases bracketing his mouth suggested he'd found plenty to smile about over the years.

Mabel supposed she should pinch herself, or shake her head really hard, or find some other way to snap out of this hallucination. That's probably what this was, she concluded, realizing she'd skipped lunch. If she squinted at just the right angle she'd see it wasn't Sam at all, but someone she knew who looked enough like him to—

"I want a divorce," Ashley growled before losing herself to another contraction, her eyes screwed shut, her teeth bared.

Mabel wrenched her attention back to Ashley, leaving the Sam-or-not question aside for now. As the expectant mother groaned, the manager returned with armfuls of throw blankets and decorative pillows, all with the tags still on.

When Ashley's contraction subsided, Mabel gently swept the hair off her sweaty forehead and spoke in a gentle tone.

"Is this your first baby?"

Ashley shook her head. "Second. I don't know what I was thinking."

"Any complications with that one?"

"None. She came fast, though. Six hours, start to finish."

"Looks like her little brother or sister is competing for the record. Are you feeling any pressure?"

"Lots. It's a boy, by the way." Ashley flashed her a brief, happy smile that reassured Mabel even more than the knowledge she'd already had one uncomplicated—if swift—delivery, so was statistically likely to have a repeat performance.

"How would you feel about standing up? Maybe we can get you to hang on to this bar here."

Ashley rose shakily to her feet, and Mabel guided her to a display wall for towel rails. She yanked on one experimentally and then, satisfied it wouldn't give way, urged Ashley to hold on. With Ashley's okay, she draped the biggest blanket across her back to give her privacy, and then asked her husband to discreetly remove his wife's underwear. Her midwife's instinct told her this baby was imminent—a suspicion instantly confirmed as Ashley groaned in a way that signaled she was almost ready to push.

She turned back to Maybe Sam, who, she concluded gloomily on second glance, was Definitely Sam.

He was also Inexplicably Sam. What on earth had brought him back to the hometown he hadn't visited since the day he left for college?

That was one of a thousand questions flashing in her mind as she looked at him, but like the others, it would have to wait. While she'd been settling Ashley he'd done a fantastic job of corralling the onlookers, even hanging rather lovely chenille throws at both ends of the aisle to block rubberneckers while leaving the way clear for the first responders—whenever they managed to beat the pouring rain and rush-hour traffic to get here. She didn't really need him for anything else—but if she sent him away, would she ever see him again?

Did it matter?

"I have advanced first aid training," he offered, as if he knew she needed a reason to keep him around. "And I attended a birth once. In the field."

"The field," she echoed, trying to ignore the uncanny way he was still able to read her, still preternaturally capable of sensing what she needed. She didn't want to think about that, or whether he meant a cow field or a daisy field or a freaking battlefield. The store manager had vanished, potentially on a quest to better color coordinate the array of linens, and she could use whatever pair of hands she could find.

Even if they belonged to Sam Strauss.

"See if you can get these blankets open." She tossed him a couple that had plastic tags keeping them folded. With her foot she shoved another one on the floor between Ashley's legs.

Ashley's moans were primal now, so fast and intense that she'd given up cursing at her husband, who by now was white-faced and wide-eyed as he stroked his wife's back.

When the next contraction finished Ashley glanced sideways at Mabel, her expression desperate. "I don't think I can do this."

"Of course you can," Mabel replied cheerfully. "And anyway, what other options do you have right now?"

Ashley's next moan was anger-fueled and determined, and Mabel smiled to herself.

Nearly there.

Mabel ordered Sam to stand behind Ashley's husband, then carefully rolled up the blanket.

"The head is right there," she reported. "Another push and it'll be out. You've got this."

Mabel crouched behind Ashley, totally focused as she prepared to guide this brand-new person earthside.

This was her favorite part of every birth. It reminded her of taking a breath before jumping into a pool, that last-second inhalation, the final step before trading the safety of dry land for the exhilarating uncertainty of the water. A new life was imminent, on the brink of bursting into the world, and there was nothing left to do but breathe, hope, and pray.

Ashley pushed, practically silent with the effort, her knuckles white on the towel rail. Her husband patted her shoulder faintly, staring down the length of her back. Sam was motionless beside him, his eyes narrowed in focus, palpably vigilant.

Mabel closed her eyes for a single second and thought, as she always did, of her biblical predecessors, Shiphrah and Puah, who defied Pharaoh to protect a generation of Hebrew sons. She recalled their courage, let it fill her heart, and opened her eyes with renewed bravery and confidence.

One final, unholy shriek from Ashley, and it was done. The baby boy slid into Mabel's hands, ruddy and blinking and hollering in fury.

Mabel quickly checked his vitals and then handed him to Ashley. Sam hastily assembled a nest of blankets from the stack he'd unpackaged and Ashley's husband eased her down into it. Mabel helped Ashley tuck the new baby beneath the neckline of her dress, checked there was enough slack in the cord, and stood back with her hands on her hips, pleased with the scene before her.

Ashley smiled up at her, twin streaks of tears splicing her cheeks. "Thank you."

"Sister, you did all the work. I just—"

A thundering crash cut her off, followed what sounded like a herd of elephants pushing a giant roller skate. An instant later Sam's cleverly hung screen was swept aside and two paramedics raced toward them with a stretcher between them—and a pack of curious shoppers following closely behind.

"You missed the main event, but I'll catch you up. Baby

boy is full-term at forty weeks and three days. Initial Apgar was nine, and—"

"Mabel?"

Was she being haunted by the ghosts of ex-boyfriends past, present, and future? Mabel turned slowly toward the other paramedic, praying it wasn't that awful guy who'd taken her to the seafood place last month—and then sighed in relief.

"Jonah," she greeted her friend Ellie's boyfriend warmly. "Fancy meeting you here."

"Heard some rock star midwife delivered a baby in the bathroom aisle. Also, I need some light switch covers. Don't suppose you've seen any?"

"Can't say I have, but then I was slightly distracted by a medical emergency."

"Which you handled more than capably." He smiled approvingly. "We'll take it from here, and you can get back to your shopping."

"Actually I'm going to hightail it out of here before they charge me for all the blankets." She nodded to the pile, now abandoned as Ashley and her newborn were safely on the stretcher.

"I saw the store manager—he seems pretty happy. I'd say there's a gift card with your name on it."

Mabel said goodbye to Jonah, and then to Ashley, who looked so calm and contented it was hard to believe she'd just given birth in the middle of a hardware store. Mabel gave the husband her number, just in case the paramedics needed any more details from the birth.

Then it was time for the task she'd been avoiding: Sam. Why was he back? For how long? Probably wasn't any of her business, but she wanted to know regardless, if only so she could studiously avoid him until he left again.

She turned toward where he'd been leaning against one of the shelving brackets, her shoulders squared, bright smile in place.

He was gone.

"Of course," she muttered, unsure whether she was more disgusted with him or herself. She'd been foolish to even entertain the notion that anything had changed in the last twelve years. He'd left her then—no surprise that he'd left her now, too.

She started toward the door, coaching herself to focus on the win. She'd delivered a healthy, happy baby in pretty damn trying circumstances. Ashley and her husband—she hadn't even bothered learning his name, she realized with a wry smile—now had a cozy family of four. One girl, one boy. A perfect balance—exactly what she used to hope for, back when she thought that future might be possible for her, too.

She could see sunlight as she approached the entrance. The rain had stopped, and the clouds had parted. She'd coaxed another new life into the world, safe and sound.

No way would she let the ghost of Sam Strauss steal her

joy.

Especially not now, with less than two weeks left before Rosh Hashanah. The date happened to coincide with the six-month anniversary of her divorce, and she'd promised herself a new start this year—a real one.

No more dating. No more swiping through apps, no more awkward text exchanges, no more stilted conversations over lukewarm coffee, no more carefully worded rejections, and absolutely no more obsessive phone-checking only to be ghosted for the umpteenth time.

No more searching, or chasing, or hoping at all. Every man she'd ever loved had left. She was done running after men who didn't deserve her. The one who was meant to be hers—if he existed at all—would walk straight toward her.

She'd been so absorbed in her thoughts, she hadn't noticed the crowd outside the store—not until she practically walked headfirst into a TV camera.

Suddenly she was surrounded. Reporters from local TV stations thrusting microphones toward her, hordes of faceless observers filming her on their phones, and a raft of store employees applauding and cheering. She was startled, excited, and feeling distinctly unmoored.

This was what she'd been waiting for.

Chapter Two

SAM HAD SURVIVED bomb blasts, mortar attacks, and a particularly gnarly earthquake, but his urge to flee had never been as strong as when he stumbled into the throng of people outside the hardware store.

Unfortunately the car accident that put his beloved career on hold three months earlier meant he'd never been less able to run.

He froze in place just outside the door, his brain working feverishly to find the quickest escape from what felt like a thousand—but was probably less than ten—phones held aloft, their camera lenses pointed straight at him.

"Hi there, did you see the baby being born inside? Do you know what happened?" Now there was a microphone in his face, and he recognized one of the local six o'clock news reporters on the other end of it.

He'd had hours of media training and had addressed a range of global news outlets in more press conferences than he could remember, often justifying to hostile journalists the perceived failure or unnecessary interference of the United Nations aid agency where he worked.

So there was absolutely no excuse for him to look down at the microphone, back up at the reporter, and mutter, "Uh-huh."

The reporter's eyes lit up and Sam immediately held up his palms, desperately trying to backpedal his affirmative response. "I mean, I know there was a baby. Beyond that…"

He caught movement in his peripheral vision and realized Mabel had just appeared a few feet to his right.

Seeing her again wasn't even slightly less painful than the first time. If anything he felt worse, as the fresh guilt of leaving her inside the store tangled with all the old wounds and unhealed heartbreak.

She was more beautiful than he'd allowed himself to remember, her glossy black hair trimmed to jaw length, her dark eyes bright and alive beneath thick lashes. Her body was more womanly than the version he'd panted over—curvier, softer—and her straight back and easy smile exuded confidence and self-assurance.

Yet her ring finger was bare—and he hated himself for checking.

For the millionth time since he saw her jogging up the bathroom aisle his stomach twisted with a nauseating mix of wistful regret and an unquenchable urge to run as fast and far as he could. The way he'd felt about her in high school had terrified him into action, and apparently a twelve-year absence hadn't diluted his response one bit.

"Well, this is turning into quite the birthday for the little guy inside." Mabel addressed the crowd in general, sounding slightly bemused.

Attention shifted to her in a single, collective motion that reminded him of a flock of ducks racing toward a floating bread crust. He waited for the reporter to swing her microphone over to Mabel, then dove to his left but it was too late. Mabel had sidled across the gap between them and she closed her hand on his arm, yanking him back to her side.

Her grip was tight and unfriendly, and totally thwarted his attempt to avoid the cameras.

He liked it anyway.

"Mom and baby are doing just fine," she was saying to the TV reporter, her charming, breezy tone belying the way her fingers dug into his forearm.

She shared a high-level version of the story, preserving Ashley's privacy. The reporter's eyes lit up when she realized Mabel was a midwife, and she began asking questions Sam suspected would add color to a six o'clock broadcast. For her part, Mabel gave her exactly the descriptive, lighthearted anecdotes Sam could see the reporter wanted.

Clever girl, he thought, a discomfiting combination of pride and affection warming his chest. Mabel's cheerful, optimistic disposition made her easy to underestimate, when in fact she was one of the smartest, most strategic people he'd ever known.

"And can you tell us a little bit about yourself?" the reporter asked.

"Absolutely." Mabel released his arm, evidently satisfied he wouldn't run away again. She guessed right—not only was his path now blocked by several latecomer police cars, standing for this long had his leg and back aching so badly he'd be lucky if he made it back to his car without limping.

"I'm a practicing midwife and the director of midwifery services at Josephine Baker Hospital in Orchard Hill, and I'm a huge advocate for choice when it comes to giving birth. My goal is for all people who give birth to feel supported and comfortable, regardless of the method of delivery, gender identity, or socioeconomic status. That said, I wouldn't normally recommend my patients deliver in a hardware store, but as long as everyone is healthy and happy, I consider it a win."

"Fantastic," the reporter said, but Sam could tell she was less enthused by Mabel's pitch.

Apparently Mabel sensed this, too, because when the reporter turned to him and asked about his role in the birth, she looped her elbow through his with a laugh.

"Believe it or not, this is my ex-boyfriend. We hadn't seen each other in more than ten years and then there he was, ripping the tags off blankets to wrap up the newborn baby."

He looked at her sharply, but it was too late—the reporter knew a compelling story when she heard one.

"Really," she said, swinging the microphone his way again. "Can you tell us who you are and what happened today?"

"Uh, well, my name is Sam Strauss, and I…"

Made decisions I'm not proud of. Loved the woman next to me more than I want to admit. Hurt her more than I can bear to remember. Did what I had to do for us both, no matter how painful.

"I just got some blankets, like she said. Mabel did all the work."

"And is she actually your ex-girlfriend?"

His jaw tightened. "Yes."

He steeled himself against whatever the reporter's next question might be, but at that moment the doors behind him swished open again. The paramedics appeared pushing Ashley and her newborn on a stretcher, her husband tagging along behind.

The reporter dashed forward, her cameraman hurrying at her heels. Within a few seconds all of the attention was on the delighted-looking new mother, and Sam knew this was his chance to leave.

Mabel knew it, too, because she rounded on him, her eyes iceberg-cold and just as hard.

"Don't you dare run off without talking to me."

Sam shifted his weight in a vain attempt to relieve the throbbing pain in his leg. "I won't."

"What are you doing here, Sam?" she demanded.

"Buying a new towel rack. The screws rusted in the old one."

She punched him in the arm—hard.

He bit back a smile. He deserved that.

"My grandmother died a couple of months ago," he told her honestly. "She spent the last few years in a memory-care facility, and her house sat empty. My dad didn't want to deal with it, so I'm fixing it up to put it on the market."

"Oh. Sorry to hear that." She ducked her chin, suitably chastened—then popped it back up. "So your plan was to sneak back to the hometown you haven't visited in twelve years, freshen up your grandmother's house, put it up for sale, and then slither out of here without letting anyone know you'd been?"

He didn't have much of a plan at all, other than a desperate need to escape the stifling silence between the four walls of his apartment in DC, but now that she mentioned it…

He tilted his head. "I hadn't intended to slither, necessarily."

"It's all a big joke to you, isn't it?" She shook her head, her effort to seem disgusted thinned by her palpable disappointment.

"No. It's not," he told her seriously. "It's just—I don't know what to say to you, Mabel. I wasn't expecting this."

"'I'm sorry' might be a good place to start."

"You know I am," he said quietly, but she shook her head.

"I know nothing about you. Maybe I thought I did once,

but now? You're a complete stranger."

That hurt far more than the fist in his arm. He couldn't disagree—they hadn't exchanged a single word in over a decade—yet some selfish, secret part of him had always remained hopeful. Not that they'd recover what they'd lost—what he'd thrown away—but that they might find a route to something new, even if it was only a pale imitation of the past.

"Well," she said, the word a thinly disguised goodbye. "Enjoy the rest of your time in town."

"Can I get your number?"

He wasn't sure who was more shocked by his impulsive, blurted request: him or Mabel. He cringed, wondering what the hell had gotten hold of him, and braced himself for her scathing response.

He waited for her to sneer. To laugh in his face. To simply turn her back and walk away.

Instead, after several moments spent studying him with a bewildered expression, she said, "Okay."

"You don't have to give it to me," he backpedaled.

"I know. Hand me your phone."

He pulled it out of his pocket, unlocked the screen, and passed it over.

She held it up, indicating the picture of a rocky, terracotta-colored landscape beneath an azure-blue sky set as his background. "Where is this?"

He hesitated, pursing his lips. "Syria," he admitted after a second.

She arched a brow, but thankfully refrained from asking any follow-up questions as she started tapping the screen. He breathed a little more easily. The last thing he wanted to do right now was stand in a rain-soaked parking lot trying to explain his exciting career path—and its temporary suspension.

"There you go." She gave the phone back and he pocketed it without looking at what she'd entered. It didn't matter. She hadn't slapped him, so he was calling this a win.

"Thanks. I won't be in town much longer, but I thought… Just in case…"

"Whatever. Call me, or don't. Makes no difference to me."

He nodded. All things considered, she'd been more than fair.

"I'm going to check on Ashley before I leave. Good luck selling the house."

"Thanks. It was nice to see you again, Mabel."

"Bye, Sam."

Without a second's hesitation she turned and walked off. He watched her for longer than he should, but she never looked back, never so much as glanced over her shoulder.

Not that he should expect otherwise after twelve years.

Not after the way he left.

He shoved his hands in his pockets and squinted up at the early-autumn sky, still pale gray, but dry. The clouds were thinning. Soon it'd be clear enough for the sun to make a final appearance before it slid below the horizon.

Funny, when he'd looked up and found Mabel at his elbow there in the bathroom aisle, he'd had the sense of a beginning. As if fate had decided to be uncharacteristically benevolent, and in the midst of so much strife—the car accident, his professional question marks, those dismal, immobile, painful months cooped up in his apartment—he was being given a chance to fix the biggest mistake he'd ever made.

But as the distance between him and Mabel increased, he knew that'd been nothing more than false optimism.

He turned in the opposite direction, mindful of his aching leg and hip and back, and gingerly made his way to his car.

This wasn't a fresh start. Just one more ending.

MABEL BALANCED THE rectangular cake in one hand while she unlocked the heavy steel door beside the shuttered flower shop where her mother had started as a part-time employee and which she now owned outright. She jogged up the stairs and let herself into the two-bedroom apartment that had been her home since her father left twenty-five years ago, and she dexterously opened the door with one hand.

"Hey, Mom, you won't believe the afternoon I had.

Thankfully I got to the bakery right before they closed. I think Elaine made it extra big for you—this thing is huge. Just remember, I will be glad to take any leftovers off your hands."

Mabel carefully placed the cake on the counter, pleased that she'd managed to get it all the way down the street and up the stairs without smudging the purple icing that read *Happy Retirement Vera*. Then she opened the fridge, took out a disc of Edam cheese, and followed the sound of the TV into the family room as she pried the cheese out of its foil-and-wax wrapping.

"Is Vera looking forward to—oh, crap."

Her mom was perched on the edge of the couch, her face white as a sheet. Mabel saw herself on the screen, but that's not why her mom was staring intently at the news broadcast.

Her attention was fixed solely on Sam Strauss.

Suddenly Mabel was in high school again, dropping Sam's hand and walking ten feet behind him as they passed the flower shop, putting fake marching-band practices on the calendar so they had time to spend together, and casually informing her mom she'd be going to prom with a big group of friends when in fact Sam had filled her locker with balloons and written the sweetest, most heartfelt note she'd ever read asking her to be his date.

Her mom still didn't know about that last one. Prom was a touchy subject, so wrapped in the drama that predated her and Sam that Mabel barely dared to mention the word throughout her adolescence.

The story of Leo Strauss—Sam's dad—and her mom, Norma, seemed to be general knowledge in Orchard Hill. The two of them were high-school sweethearts and local darlings, the baseball star and the valedictorian, destined for paired greatness.

Except in their senior year they'd had a fight. Nothing significant—something to do with conflicting plans for afterprom parties, Norma had told her—and in typically dramatic teenage fashion, they'd broken up.

Eager to make Leo jealous, Norma quickly arranged a new date for the prom: Joel Antonoff, who was charming and rebellious and already well known to local law enforcement.

He was also Mabel's father.

Not to be outdone, Leo pivoted in the other direction. He asked out Evelyn Horowitz, the beautiful, beloved, and practically perfect salutatorian who'd been nipping at Norma's social heels since they were freshmen.

Norma and Leo turned up to the prom with their respective rival dates on their arms—only to spend the entire evening together. What most of Orchard Hill didn't know—but Mabel did—was that they'd spent that time working through their issues and joyfully reconciling. Neither wanted to hurt their dates' feelings, though, so they agreed to continue the night separately, and then let Joel and Evelyn down gently in a day or so.

A fine plan—until fate intervened.

Leo and Evelyn were just blocks from her house when a pedestrian unexpectedly stepped off the sidewalk and into the gutter. Thinking the man was about to cross the street in front of their car, Leo panicked, swerved out of the way and into oncoming traffic. Another car hit them and they spun, the vehicle finally coming to rest when it smashed against a tree on the passenger side.

Except for a few cuts and bruises, Leo was remarkably unscathed.

Evelyn spent three weeks in a coma.

Neither Mabel nor Sam knew exactly what their parents had said to each other in the days following the accident, but their very existences were evidence of the outcome.

Leo gave up his baseball scholarship to stay local and help Evelyn through her rehab. They got married, promptly had their first son, Zach, and then Sam was born a couple years later.

Norma left town as planned, earning her degree from a small, liberal-arts college in Pennsylvania. She and Joel dated off and on, and when she moved home after her father was diagnosed with cancer, they were on for real. She got pregnant, they went to the courthouse, and seven years to the day after the accident, Mabel was born.

Mabel often wondered why God had thrust her and Sam together when their fleeting happiness brought so much heartbreak. Despite marrying other people, neither Norma nor Leo seemed able to move on from their ill-fated high-school relationship, and their agonized yearning hovered like a ghost in the background whenever they were in the same place together—which wasn't often.

Attending the same temple meant they'd always been faint acquaintances, but when she and Sam began to hang out in the same friend group in middle school, his parents were unequivocal: if he was caught with that fatherless hussy Mabel Antonoff, there'd be hell to pay. For her part Norma was stoic, and didn't explicitly forbid Mabel from seeing Sam, but her cold, severe disapproval had been clear whenever she saw them together—like right now, on the evening news.

"What's going on, Mabel?" her mother asked. Norma was usually trusting to a fault, but now her words practically dripped with suspicion.

"Would it be enough to say I had an eventful afternoon?" Mabel attempted a joking smile, but her mother's stern look wiped it off her face.

She sighed and took a seat on the couch beside her mom.

"The short version is that a woman went into labor at the hardware store and I assisted with the birth. The longer version is that Sam Strauss is back in town, putting his grandmother's house up for sale. He was in the store at the same time, and he helped me. A little."

Norma drew breath for what Mabel bet was a raft of follow-up questions, so she held up her palms to stave off her mom.

"That's all I know, I swear. We barely exchanged twenty words, and they were the first ones we've spoken to each other since he left for college."

Now Norma's lips thinned, undoubtedly remembering that day with the same clarity Mabel did. She reached over and patted her daughter's arm, sympathy softening her expression.

"I guess that must've been a shock, seeing him again after so long. Did he…say anything?"

"Like sorry? No. But to be fair, I had my hands full. The whole thing was awkward. I think we were both glad to walk away from each other."

Her mother nodded, evidently satisfied with that fib.

Truth was, Mabel hadn't stopped thinking about Sam since the moment she turned her back on him. She brimmed with questions and regrets and second-guesses, wondering if she should've been friendlier, more receptive, willing to hear him out. That was probably her last chance to get closure and she'd cut it short, so intent on showing him how little he mattered that she hadn't thought about what she wanted—or needed.

Since then she'd played out a million alternative scenarios in her mind and conceived of endless ways she could've handled it better.

All of which amounted to exactly nothing, she thought glumly, taking one last look at Sam's handsome face on the screen before the broadcast moved on to the weather.

Her mom seemed to shake herself, as if emerging from a daydream, and turned back to Mabel with her characteristic, upbeat smile.

"You said you delivered a baby in the hardware store? Oh my goodness, Mabel. Tell me everything."

Mabel exhaled, the specters of two generations of lost loves fading, and launched into the tale.

She'd gotten as far as Sam's creation of a privacy perimeter using chenille blankets when she realized that her phone was buzzing nonstop. The first time it rang on the couch cushion beside her it had been a call from an unknown number, so she'd silenced it and put it to one side. Now it was vibrating endlessly, and when she unlocked it, the screen was clogged with notifications. Texts, emails, pings on various social media sites, and missed calls from what appeared to be everyone she'd ever known—plus a whole host of random callers, too.

"Hang on—my phone is going crazy." She frowned at the screen, trying and failing to scroll through the various alerts before new ones popped up.

"Must be the TV broadcast. Everyone wants to congratulate you," Norma said enthusiastically.

Mabel hummed thoughtfully, opening her email. Sure enough, there were a few well-wishers, but also a bunch of notes from other TV channels. And the local newspaper, and a not-quite-local newspaper, and a magazine.

Meanwhile her social-media notifications already numbered in the hundreds and climbed as she watched. She tapped into one of her accounts, discovered a hashtag containing her name, and tapped right back out.

She looked up at her mom, numb with disbelief.

"I think I'm going viral."

Norma tilted her head, evidently unfamiliar with the magnitude of that term. Mabel shook her head—her mom was great, but a social-media expert she was not—and returned her attention to her phone.

A new number appeared in the list of those trying to call, and her breath caught in her lungs.

Sam.

She popped up from the couch, ruing her excitement at hearing from him even as she unhesitatingly answered the call. "Hello?"

"Oh, good, your phone hasn't exploded from overuse."

"Not yet, but it's only a matter of time." She shot her mom an easy smile as she affected a casual wander into the kitchen. "Yours, too?"

"I'm suddenly very popular, yes. Have you seen what it's all about?"

"No, there's too much to wade through. Why?"

He paused, and then replied, "It's the ex-boyfriend comment. People are speculating—"

"I don't want to know," she interrupted him, pressing her hand over her eyes. She didn't know if it was technically possible to cringe all the way to your tendons, but that's how deep hers felt.

She could already imagine the responses. Calls for them to get back together, questions about why they broke up, women offering to take him off her hands, men promising to show her a real man…

Maybe that last part didn't sound so awful. After all, she still had a couple of weeks before Rosh Hashanah and her no-more-chasing resolution. She'd already disabled notifications on her dating apps, but would it be the worst thing in the world to switch them back on just for a couple of days, to see whether her viral fame translated to real-life romance?

At that thought Mabel bolted upright as she imagined a cartoon lightbulb switching on above her head. Of course—the opportunity was so obvious, she couldn't believe it had taken her more than a second to recognize it. Forget her romantic life—she had to use this to publicize her profession. Hadn't that been the point of talking to the media all along?

Just last year she'd moved her midwifery practice from a homey birth center to pioneer an in-hospital program at one of the smaller maternity wards in the area. Her demand from patients was almost immediate; however, the resources to serve as many as were interested were limited. For months she'd been campaigning within the hospital to invest in expanding the program, in particular to improve access for patients with lower incomes. She'd had some murmurs of interest but nothing material—until now.

Not only would a public profile as a heroic midwife do wonders for her own program, it might open doors for the development of similar services in other locations. She supposed her bosses might grumble about competition, but considering how many people they regularly turned away, and the distances some patients drove to access midwifery services, she doubted that—

"Mabel? Are you still there?"

"Yes. What were you saying?" She pinched the bridge of her nose, snapping herself back to the present.

"We need to figure out how to handle this. Do you have time to talk right now?"

She glanced at her mom, whose own phone had begun to ring, undoubtedly with friends and acquaintances who'd seen Mabel on TV. Norma's gaze drifted to hers and narrowed with curiosity.

"No," Mabel said, swiveling around so her back was to her mom.

"Are you at work?"

"No," she repeated.

"You're with your mom."

Was she really that easy to read, even twelve years later?

Or did he simply understand her like no one else ever had?

"Mmhm," she hummed affirmatively.

Another pause, this one hesitant. She waited patiently, already guessing what he was about to say, and more than happy to let him squirm.

"Would you like to come here?" he asked with the enthusiasm of a man agreeing to a complicated and drawn-out dental procedure.

"Sure," she said brightly.

He started to give her the address, but she interjected, "I know the house. I'll be right there," and hung up without waiting for a response.

Mabel sensed her mother's interest and avoided her eyes as she scooped up her bag.

"One of my first-time moms thinks she's having premature contractions. She's on my way home so I'm going to stop in and check. Elaine said to put the cake in the fridge so the frosting doesn't melt. Give my love to Vera. 'Night!"

"Wait, what about this viral thing?" Norma scrambled up from the sofa but Mabel's hand was already on the doorknob.

"Oh, I don't know. I'll figure it out. Love you!"

"Love you, too," her mom called in the instant before Mabel slipped out to the hallway. She scrambled down the stairs, around the front of the shop, and back through the passage to the alley where she'd parked.

Mabel put her car in gear and eased out to the road. She knew where Sam's grandmother's house was. She knew how to get there. She knew which streets to avoid, and where to park when she arrived.

But she had no idea what to do when she got there.

Chapter Three

SAM EASED INTO one of the lightly padded, seventies-era chairs in the kitchen, stretching his sore leg in front of him. He crossed his arms, resigned to waiting—and then spotted that morning's coffee cup beside the sink on the opposite side of the room.

He hauled himself out of the chair and made his way over to stow the mug in the dishwasher. He started back toward the table, then changed his mind, moving instead into the living room for a final once-over.

His grandparents' house was typical for this part of Orchard Hill, a long, narrow, brick-fronted townhouse built at the turn of the century. The interior was immaculate but painfully dated, and the once-elegant front room now reminded him of a funeral-parlor lobby. Heavy, darkly upholstered furniture absorbed the light afforded by the bay window, and the faded, maroon carpet managed to simultaneously muffle conversation and amplify every creaking floorboard.

No, this wasn't the right place for a conversation with Mabel. The kitchen was better. He'd just go check it one more time, make sure there were no crumbs on the counter, and maybe hide that pile of mail in a cupboard.

He'd only made it two steps when the doorbell rang. He cursed under his breath, inhaled slowly, and swung around to open it.

Mabel stood framed in the doorway, the outside light casting a golden gleam on her dark hair. In that moment he was seventeen again, arranging clandestine, logistically complex meetings tied into visits to his grandparents so his mom and dad wouldn't know he'd spent a chunk of his absence with her.

He wished he could tell her how much she'd meant to him back then, that she'd been his only emotional outlet as he came of age in a household thick with silent tension. That she was the one person who let him talk and never shamed him for how he felt, and who showed him the potential for love to exist in his otherwise loveless world—even if that love was exactly what sent him running.

Instead he said, "Hi. Thanks for coming over."

"No problem." She breezed past him into the front room, kicked off her shoes, and flopped onto the ancient pool-table-green chaise longue beneath the bay window.

So much for his agonizing over the perfect setting. He shut the door and followed her, trying to minimize the stiffness in his gait. He lowered himself carefully into the wingback chair across from her and threaded his fingers in his lap.

"Let's get this out of the way," she began, characteristically unhesitating. "Are you still the same asshole who dumped me twelve years ago or have you grown up since then? Just so I know who I'm dealing with."

He knew this moment would come, and he'd prepared himself, but her acid tone made him shift with discomfort nonetheless.

"I'm sorry about the way I ended things," he told her, and he was.

He also had no intention of telling her the whole truth.

There was no point. Total honesty wouldn't change the past, and it wouldn't repair the damage. It would only give her one more reason to despise his parents, and he'd wasted enough of his life processing his bitterness toward them. No need to spread that poison any farther than it had to go.

He'd take this one on his shoulders alone. He'd carried it this far, and it was a weight he deserved.

"You remember that night," he said, a statement rather than a question.

She nodded, her gaze hollowing, and he knew she recalled that time as vividly as he did. Those final weeks of the summer after their senior year, the slow, sluggish countdown to the day he left for college, and she stayed behind.

The thick, still, late-August heat. Their constant need for each other, the gnawing hunger made sharp-edged by their impending separation and the opacity of the future. The mounting pressure in both their houses as their parents grew hawkeyed and suspicious, their adolescent deception thinning as desperation made them sloppy and frantic.

And the heavy, humid night it all unraveled. Silent lightning splitting the sky, bare flesh, salty and slick. He'd spread a quilt on the unvarnished, splintery floorboards. She'd sighed against his neck, murmuring his name. Afterward they lay together for a long time, limbs tangled, breaths slowing, hearts beating in tandem.

To this day he didn't know what prompted his mother to leave her air-conditioned bedroom at one o'clock in the morning, make her way downstairs and outside, and climb the rickety wooden steps to the unfinished room over their garage. He'd never forget her horrified expression, though, or the disgusting accusations she'd hurled at Mabel, or the urgent thumping of his father's footsteps as he ran to investigate the commotion.

He'd done his best to protect Mabel that night. He'd wrapped her in the quilt and held her close, glaring at his parents in defiant silence, tucking her head beneath his chin as she wept hot tears against his chest, but it wasn't enough.

His father snatched Mabel away and ushered her down the stairs. His mother threw her clothes into the backyard. His father's car roared to life in the garage. Then his mother returned, crossed the room, and slapped him so hard his ears rang.

He'd spent the next several hours perched on the edge of his bed, enduring his mother's semihysterical berating and empty threats—they wouldn't pay his college tuition, they'd kick him out of the house, they'd never speak to him again, a litany of flimsy attempts to regain control of the now eighteen-year-old son she was on the brink of losing to adulthood. He'd been stoic, silent but immovable in his commitment to Mabel. Soon he'd be in another state, and although the distance from Mabel disconcerted him, it felt liberating, too. Even if they weren't physically close, they'd finally be free from interference in their relationship.

"My mom lost her mind, as you can imagine. I ignored most of it, but the more I thought about it, the more I realized that on some level she had a point. College should be a fresh start, a unique opportunity for reinvention. That's why I wanted to talk to you the next day."

Half a lie—his mom had made that argument. But it was what his dad said to him after his mom left, the way he'd closed the bedroom door, his imploring tone of voice, that prompted Sam to do what came next.

"Let her go, Sam," his dad had said, gruffly, quietly, hands clasped so tightly in his lap his knuckles were white. "You'll ruin her life like I ruined your mother's."

Mabel exhaled, drawing him out of that stuffy, too-small bedroom and back to the present.

"You mean when you met me in the middle-school parking lot to break up with me," she said flatly.

He cringed inwardly, the memory of their breakup so vivid he could feel the heat reflecting on the asphalt, hear the heavy clank of the service door as a member of the maintenance staff pushed through it, and see every nuance in her expression as it shifted from disbelief to anguish to quiet, dignified resignation.

"I could've handled it a lot better. No excuses. I'm sorry, Mabel."

She glowered at him, and he could tell she wanted to fight. She probably had a decade of pent-up anger and frustration and hurt she was itching to take out on him, and on some level he hoped she would. He'd never be able to change what happened, but if screaming or throwing something at him made her feel better, it might alleviate some of his guilt, too.

But evidently he wasn't the only one who'd changed over the years. Mabel didn't hurl the tasseled cushion at his head, or shout until her voice went scratchy, or even fix him with the hot, furious stare he used to dread. She simply took a deep breath, closed her eyes, and let it out slowly.

And if he was honest with himself, he was a little disappointed.

"It was a long time ago," she said tersely. She reopened her eyes and focused on him, her expression softening almost imperceptibly.

"I know your folks moved that fall, while you were at college. What else? What did you grow up and do with your life, Sam Strauss?"

He allowed himself a small smile and hoped she didn't

take it the wrong way. "International aid. Eight years with a refugee agency."

"Wow. I'm happy for you—genuinely. Do you enjoy it?"

"Every minute. Right now I'm…taking a break, but I should be back in action soon."

She arched a brow, and he could practically hear the questions piling up in her mind, but to his immense relief she left them unasked.

"I hope it all works out for you."

"Thanks." He shifted in his seat, awkwardness vying with curiosity. There was so much he wanted to know about her life since they parted. She'd become a midwife—an impressively capable one, at that. Did she live alone? Did she have a boyfriend? Had anyone ever loved her as wholly and purely as he had?

Or broken her heart as brutally?

"How about you?" he asked, cringing inwardly at how stiff that question sounded.

"Well, I still live in Orchard Hill. Not quite as exciting as wherever your job takes you, although there was some controversy last year when the pizza place got a liquor license." She offered a hint of a teasing smile. "Otherwise my life is pretty mundane. Work, sleep, pretending I'll finally start using my gym membership. Now, should we talk about our fifteen minutes of Internet fame?"

"I think we should ignore it," he said.

"I think we should leverage it," she said at the same time.

"Leverage it for what?" he asked cautiously, a knot of dread already tightening in his stomach.

"I don't know what you've got going on, but I've spent months trying to convince the hospital system where I work to expand their midwifery services to more locations. That's my cause in general, I guess you could say—accessible birth options. And I'll never have another platform like this one to get my message across."

"Sounds like a great idea," he told her earnestly, genuinely pleased—if unsurprised—that she'd found her passion and become its relentless advocate. "Good luck with it. But I'm going to duck out and hope it all blows over."

"You can't."

"Why not?" he asked slowly, already certain he wouldn't like the answer.

"Let's be real—no one cares about the baby. They want to know about us, our history, and whether this is the start of some grand love story."

He wished he could disagree, but he couldn't—not honestly. It's why he called her in the first place. The clip of her grabbing his arm and remarking that she'd just been assisted by her long-lost ex-boyfriend seemed to be the image that launched a thousand comments. He thought if they worked together they might be more effective in shutting it all down, figuring the last thing either of them wanted was to be associated with each other in such an enormously public way.

Apparently not.

Regardless, appearing in any capacity in the media was so far out of the realm of possibility in his mind that he dismissed it without a second thought. After the accident he wanted nothing more than to withdraw for a while, to lick his wounds, to rest and recuperate and find his way back to the high-octane, untethered life he'd enjoyed before.

That's why he'd offered to come down to Orchard Hill and get the empty house ready for sale. Days spent alone in an empty house, quietly toiling at minor renovations, clearing out decades of clutter, with no need to speak to anyone save the occasional cashier at the grocery store. The perfect setting to try to calm his derailed nerves, reconnect with his irrepressible former self, maybe say a few goodbyes to the life—and people—he'd left so abruptly, and shake off the lingering, nagging bite of loneliness and self-doubt that hadn't let go since they'd slapped that hospital bracelet on his wrist.

Because as much as he hated to admit it to himself, that driver had flattened more than his bike and his leg on that muggy afternoon, just blocks from his apartment in Washington, DC. He'd lost something else beneath the wheels of that car, something he didn't quite have a name for, which bound together his courage and his optimism and his once-infinite sense of the possible.

He wanted to get it back. He *had* to. He couldn't do his job without it, couldn't fling himself into conflict while this uncomfortable sense of isolation kept tugging his shirtsleeve, pulling him backward.

So he figured he'd go to the source—his long-abandoned hometown of Orchard Hill, where he'd had a community and connections he could barely imagine now. The place he'd learned to be a friend, a confidant, and a lover—to tie up his life with someone else's and enjoy the tension of their pull, not fear it. The epicenter of who he'd been before his decision to wall himself off from any of the life-ruining emotions that might make him vulnerable, and to keep his undeserving heart tightly in check, no matter how constantly it ached for the woman he'd never forgotten, or how even now the slightest motion of her tongue over her lips made it clench and skip and stagger.

Somewhere out there he'd gotten lost. If he could go back to the beginning—back to who he'd been at his best—maybe he could find his way again.

But under Mabel's scrutiny, silently calling him to account as the yellowish light from the old lamp lit twin fires in her clear eyes, he felt more adrift than ever.

"Do it, then," he told her, deciding his first priority right now had to be getting her out of here before he lost his bearings completely. "You can talk about us without me. You have my full permission. You're even welcome to make me the villain."

"You are the villain," she said, deadpan.

He stared at her, trying to decide whether she was joking.

"All these interview requests are for both of us." She unlocked her phone, tapped the screen, and passed it over. "See? They're hoping for a romantic reunion story from a cute couple, not some harridan midwife atop her soapbox."

He glanced down the list of emails, then handed back her phone. "Do we have a romantic reunion story to tell them?"

"Of course not, but that's not the point. We just have to *allude* to one." She drew her hands through the air in opposite directions as if concluding a magic trick.

He wanted to help her—more than anything, he wanted just a fraction of redemption in her estimation—but he thought of the clump of cell phones outside the hardware store, imagined the bright light of a TV camera, and swallowed against a wave of nausea.

"I'm sorry, Mabel, but I'm not at a point right now where I'd be comfortable going on TV to talk about anything, never mind fib about my relationship status. By all means, use my name and our story and say whatever you want. But I'm out."

"Listen to me, Sam Strauss," she commanded, her tone suddenly as sharp and cold as stainless steel.

In an instant she was off the chaise longue and looming over him—to the extent that anyone with her diminutive stature could loom.

"You owe me," she told him, her index finger barely an inch from his face. "You've owed me for a long time, and

I'm calling it in. You will do these interviews with me. You will smile, and be charming, and say whatever you have to for us to stay in front of the camera long enough for me to shill for midwifery services, do you hear me?"

He studied her through narrowed eyes. Her expression was a convincing mask of threat and intimidation, but he knew her, and even after all these years he could read what she probably thought she'd hidden.

She was angry, sure. Furious, even. Obstinate, vengeful, demanding—all of those igniting qualities that fueled her fire-starter personality and incendiary temper.

None of which made a dent on him twelve years ago, and were equally ineffective now.

But there was something else flickering in her dark eyes—something small, and soft, and scared.

He leaned forward, instantly hooked, desperate for a closer look, but she jerked backward, regarding him with hostility.

"One interview," he decided aloud. "Your choice. I'll play along with whatever you want, but then I'm done."

"One is pointless. We have to build momentum. That'll take five, at least."

"Absolutely not. I won't even be here that long."

That knocked her off balance, and some of the chill left her voice. "When are you leaving?"

"As soon as the house is sold, or to a point where I can handle the sale remotely. It'll be on the market for Rosh

Hashanah, and I need to be out of here by Yom Kippur at the latest."

"Rosh Hashanah is less than two weeks away."

He shrugged.

"Three interviews, then. We can fit those in before the holiday."

"I don't know, Mabel," he said, groping for another reason to decline—and finding one. "Have you thought about how this will affect our parents? Your mom, my dad?"

For a split second her expression darkened, and he knew that despite the many years in between she still carried the guilt and uneasiness he did with their long-running deception. They'd been good kids, unused to lying, but more than that, they'd known all along that the wound of Norma and Leo's split had never healed.

They didn't need confirmation in the wistful way Leo looked at Norma from across the room at Oneg Shabbat, or in the box of decades-old love letters that Norma kept under her bed. They heard it in the way Leo and Norma said each other's names, in their matching refusals to discuss what happened, and in their dire, pleading warnings to their children to stay away from each other.

The shadow behind her eyes passed. "They're grown-ups. They can deal with it. Anyway, it's only short-term, and we're not promising anything—just fueling speculation. It's not like we're getting married."

"I suppose," he grudgingly agreed. Then he looked up

suddenly, realizing she probably hadn't heard, not without his grandmother to keep the Orchard Hill community informed. "My parents got divorced two years ago."

"I had no idea," she told him, visibly shocked.

Sam lifted a shoulder. "It was a long time coming. You know what they were like when we were young. It never got better. My mom left, moved to California, started over. She went back to school and became a licensed counselor, if you can believe that."

Her mouth twisted in sympathy. Mabel was the only person in the world who understood the way he'd grown up, the veneer of polite respectability that concealed an atmosphere of constant tension, withheld emotions, and hostile silence. He'd never been able to explain it to anyone else—but then again, he'd never tried overly hard.

"Good luck to her patients," she said wryly.

"I know. To be fair, they're both a lot happier now, and nicer people as a result," he said truthfully, a fact that provided yet another nail in the coffin of his optimism about his romantic future. His parents were miserable during their marriage, and borderline delightful now they were divorced. What more proof did he need?

"Good for them, I guess," Mabel replied. "Anyway, if anyone gets their feelings hurt seeing us sitting next to each other, they'll have to get over it. After all, they got what they wanted, didn't they?"

He looked down at his hands, clasped in his lap. She was

right. They'd won.

And he'd been complicit.

"Two interviews, and they have to be done before Rosh Hashanah. Final offer."

"Deal." She grinned. "Pleasure doing business with you."

He grunted disagreeably, rising from his chair with a concerted effort to stifle his grimace as his back complained at the movement.

"I'll go through the invitations and choose the two that seem highest-profile. Then I'll give you a call and we can coordinate our story. Sound like a plan?"

"I guess," he replied, already regretting his assent to this wild idea. Hopefully she was overestimating the public interest in the two of them, and this would all be settled with a couple of five-minute slots on unwatched, local, daytime newscasts.

Still, he supposed he'd have to get a haircut.

He followed Mabel to the door, certain it was only an illusion that the room seemed to dim in her wake, as if she were a source of light all on her own.

"Thanks for going along with this. I know it probably seems ridiculous to you, after everything you've done, but down here in the trenches even a little exposure goes a long way."

"It's fine," he told her, avoiding her eyes, discomfort tangling with embarrassment and guilt. Time wasn't all that separated them now. He'd graduated from his elite college, worked for a global nonprofit, and traveled all over the world.

He couldn't know everywhere Mabel had been since he last saw her, but he had a hunch most of it wasn't all that far from where they stood.

"Cool. I'll be in touch."

He reached around her to open the door, and for a split second he was close enough to hear her breathe, to feel the soft brush of her hip against his leg, and to register her scent.

So different, and yet exactly the same, he thought, inhaling. Vanilla, creamy and smooth. Freshly peeled tangerine. Cotton blankets plucked off the washing line, light and soft and sun-warmed.

Her scent was an echo of another time, another version of their lives, one that was shared and unified. It reassured him, took his hand and squeezed it, and at the same time ripped him to shreds.

He cleared his throat, shaking himself back to the present. The door creaked on its hinges.

"Goodnight, Mabel," he managed, the words coming out gruff and stiff.

She raised her hand in farewell, took three steps down the front path—and turned back.

"I can recommend a good physical therapist, if you're interested."

Heat flared in his ears and his cheeks, and he stepped back into the shadow of the doorway, hopeful she hadn't seen.

"Thanks," he muttered, then ducked inside and shut the door before she could say another word.

He hovered out of view of the street, watching her from the gloom, feeling like the beast in the castle as she hesitated on the walkway, then continued to her car. Her headlights briefly lit the road, and then she pulled out and drove off.

He slumped into the nearest chair, scrubbing his hand over his eyes.

She'd spotted his limp.

All that pain and willpower and effort he'd put into hiding it from her, and she'd seen right through him.

But that was Mabel. She'd always seen him for exactly who he was.

What on earth was he thinking, agreeing to do these interviews with her, airing their sad story for the world to see? That's not what he needed right now, not what he'd promised himself when he'd set off on the long trip from his sleek apartment in Washington, DC, to the St. Louis suburb he'd called home.

The accident had shaken him to his core. As he spent night after lonely night in his hospital room, unvisited, uncared for, unloved, it made him question every previously rock-solid perception he'd ever had.

He'd spent most of his life managing unimaginable crises, making life-or-death choices at a moment's notice with imperfect information. He did it calmly and logically, guided always by the intention to safeguard as many people as possible to the best of his ability. He'd earned professional respect, was a valued voice in his field, and treasured the knowledge that, on balance, he wrought more good than harm.

You'd think such a worthy contributor might have someone he could call from the back of an ambulance.

He did not.

As the weeks wore on, his sense of his isolation became more acute, especially as he realized it was self-made.

Sure, he'd helped plenty of people over the years.

He'd done an even better job of shielding himself from anyone who might dare to know him.

By the time he was released from the hospital and left to his own devices in his apartment, he was rattled. Anxious. And less willing than ever to ask for help.

It wasn't difficult to persuade his dad to send him the keys to his grandmother's house—his old man had been avoiding dealing with it for years. Requesting the leave of absence from work took a little more strength, and the ease with which it was granted didn't help his dwindling sense of usefulness. When he hobbled onto the plane he wanted nothing more than to disappear for a while, to recalibrate and figure out how to start over. At the same time, maybe he could finally close the door on his life in Orchard Hill—a door that had been slammed so violently it still rattled on its hinges whenever the howling winds of his self-doubt picked up speed.

Rosh Hashanah was his deadline. What better time for a reinvention than the New Year?

Doubling down on an already disquietingly public moment with his ex-girlfriend, on the other hand, was decidedly not part of his plan.

He exhaled heavily, hauling himself up from his seat. He'd promised her now—it'd be wrong to back out. He'd have to grin and bear it all somehow.

Sam glanced at the shadowed doorway, recalling the golden glow that Mabel had seemed to carry with her, as if she toted a sunbeam in her back pocket.

Then he switched off the lights, plunging the front room into darkness.

Chapter Four

"THIS IS THE sad part—you're officially discharged from postpartum care. But that doesn't mean we don't want holiday cards, random updates, and to see your faces any time you're in the vicinity of the hospital. Understood?" Mabel asked, feigning sternness.

Her patient nodded, her eyes brimming as she hoisted her six-week-old son higher on her shoulder. "I can't thank you enough. I know I was disappointed when we had to go with a C-section, but now I'm just happy he's here and healthy."

Mabel shrugged. "Sometimes these kiddos do their own things, and that's why medical interventions like C-sections exist. Either way, you did great, and you should feel super proud for bringing this little guy earthside safely."

They exchanged a tight hug, Mabel held the baby one more time despite his skeptical expression, and then she bid her patient goodbye and picked up the chart for her next appointment.

She rapped lightly on the door, then swept in with a smile. This was a new-patient intake, and she found a still imperceptibly pregnant woman seated beside someone older she guessed was her mother.

Mabel introduced herself briefly, and then sat down to listen.

"I'm Elyse, and this is my mom, Adriana. She saw you on the news," Elyse announced with a roll of her eyes.

"I had to come and see you in person. Can you tell us what's happening with your ex-boyfriend? Are you two getting back together? What was his name again…Sam?" Adriana's eyes were wide and bright, her smile so hopeful Mabel wished she could promise her the happily-ever-after she so clearly wanted.

"We'll see," she said cagily. "Anyway, tell me about you and your hopes for this birth, Elyse."

Elyse glanced sideways at her mom, and then straightened. "I'm thirty-six, I'm a lawyer, and I'm a single mom by choice. This baby was conceived artificially using a sperm donor."

"Good for you!" Mabel exclaimed, holding up her palm for Elyse to high-five.

They talked about Elyse's preferred birth plan—minimal intervention, though she'd consider an epidural—and Mabel carefully held eye contact with her patient to avoid drawing attention to Adriana's frequent grunts of disapproval. Mabel wished Elyse had come on her own, so that she might offer her suggestions about finding a supportive birth partner or considering a doula, but she made a mental note to add that to her file so she'd remember it next time.

As they wrapped up Adriana asked, "What about you? Any kids?"

"Not yet," she replied brightly.

"And you're not married?" Mabel didn't miss the older woman's pointed glance at her bare ring finger.

"Happily divorced." She grinned.

That response usually shut down even the most well-meaning inquiries, but to her surprise, Adriana's eyes twinkled. "Might be hope for you and Sam after all."

Five minutes later Mabel dropped Elyse's chart into her to-be-written-up pile and leaned over the high desk to wait for Kim, the practice's medical assistant, to finish her phone call.

"I'm taking lunch. Be back in an hour."

Kim nodded, then groaned as the phone rang again.

"You're going to kill me with this viral thing," she admonished teasingly. "We've been getting calls all morning from potential new patients. Well, half of them are potential new patients, the other half are reporters pretending to be pregnant."

Mabel laughed. "Don't worry, I'm sure it'll all blow over soon."

"I hope so, because there's no way we can accommodate all these inquiries. Don't suppose you've convinced the higher-ups to expand our program through the whole hospital system yet, huh?" Kim tilted her head, only half joking.

"Working on it," Mabel said breezily, then pushed into the hallway, yanking out her phone as she walked. After being rendered almost totally useless by the tidal wave of notifications last night, the influx of contact from Internet randoms had slowed down—which worried her almost as much as it was a relief. She knew this kind of attention burned out as swiftly as it flared to life, and she needed to make use of it while she still could.

She scrolled through the various alerts as she wolfed down a sandwich in the hospital café, playing a publicity version of King of the Hill in which she mentally stacked her top-two interview requests until one or both of them were knocked off by something better.

She tried to focus on the task at hand, fought the urge to click on one of the frequently shared links to the video of her and Sam, and then cursed under her breath when she did it anyway.

The sound was off, but that didn't matter. She'd watched this clip at least a hundred times, and her almost hypnotic obsession with playing it on repeat had nothing to do with listening to herself extoll the virtues of midwifery.

Sam captivated her. At once joltingly familiar and unnervingly alien, she'd studied every detail of his image in the video, trying to knit together the boy she remembered and the man he'd become. For so long her primary objective was to forget about him, so giving herself permission to allow him into her thoughts felt dangerous as well as exhilarating.

Those first few weeks after the night his parents discovered them remained some of the worst of her life. Of course his parents' fury and her own mother's icy, hostile silence were awful—but his abandonment was much, much worse.

She'd never forget his face as she approached where he sat waiting for her on the long, concrete sign spelling out the name of their middle school. She knew whatever he had to tell her would be bad, but she'd never imagined just how instantly and thoroughly it'd turn her life upside down.

"I need a fresh start—maybe we both do. I don't want to be in a relationship right now," he'd said, and the world as she'd known it crumbled beneath her feet.

She had no doubt that his parents had something to do with his sudden about-face, obviously in the immediate aftermath of their midnight tryst, but also in the whole context of his life. Their simmering unhappiness seemed to infect anyone who got too close, so it made sense for Sam to be skeptical about love.

She'd just never considered that he might be skeptical about her, too.

Her transition to college had been difficult anyway—unable to scrape together sufficient funding for her dream school out of state, she reluctantly enrolled locally—and the sudden loss of the most important person in her life compounded the tumult. She was listless, melancholy, and extraordinarily lonely, scrolling through her friends' wild social-media updates as they navigated the first semester away from home. She went from graduating in the top ten in her class to barely passing, unable to stir herself to care.

Then Sam's parents left town.

She'd had to drive back and forth several times before she could believe the for-sale sign in front of his house was real. A few days later she found herself filling a floral order for delivery to Evelyn Strauss—a going-away bouquet wishing her well on their move to Connecticut.

To this day she and her mom had never discussed the abrupt departures of the two men they'd loved and lost, but when her close friend Saul Keller came home from Princeton for Thanksgiving break that year, it was the first thing she'd wanted to talk about.

"I bet it has nothing to do with you, or us, or Orchard Hill. Maybe he really does want to start over," Saul had offered kindly, their toes dragging in the sand beneath the swing set that had hosted their most significant heart-to-hearts.

She'd wept openly that night. Let Saul fold her into his arms and promise her she'd be fine. She even found the wherewithal to smile when he suggested he hunt Sam down and break both his arms, while at the same time finally allowing her heart to shatter into the pieces she'd been trying and failing to hold together.

Mabel got home from the playground and cried herself to sleep. Then she woke up the next morning and vowed to put Sam Strauss behind her forever.

She'd done a pretty good job, too. She'd blocked him everywhere she could—her phone, her email, her social-media accounts. She told her friends not to tell her anything about him, which wasn't too difficult, considering he'd ghosted all of them as well. Keeping him out of her thoughts and dreams was a little harder, but over time even his presence there receded. She went on dates, had a couple of one-night stands, and finally settled into a relationship that took her down the aisle—and then to a divorce lawyer—all with barely a moment's thought spared for the first man she'd loved.

As she replayed the video on her phone yet again, she gave herself a mental pat on the back for a more-or-less successful decade of pretending he'd never existed.

Now she just had to rebuild her entire world to include him again.

Temporarily, she told herself pointedly, finding the will-power to close out the video and stow her phone.

This was a short-term opportunity for professional advocacy. Nothing else would change, including her Rosh Hashanah resolution to put a moratorium on dating. Soon Sam would be…wherever…and she'd be looking back on this brief period with a smile.

In the meantime she had a new baby to check in on.

Mabel stopped into the hospital gift shop for a box of locally made chocolate, then set off across the lobby toward the elevators, trying to clear Sam's image from her mind. She really didn't need to run another analysis on the ways his face had changed—gaunter, more angular—or the fact that his not-quite-blue, not quite-gray eyes were exactly the same. Or that his hair looked just as thick and soft as she remembered, and was now a little overgrown, long enough to create a few curls that hung over his forehead like—

"Well, if it isn't our celebrity midwife. Haven't left us for a new career as an influencer?"

It took Mabel a couple of seconds to pull herself out of her daydream and focus on Cathy Lopez, one of the senior vice presidents in the hospital system—and a key member of the steering committee that would decide whether to expand the midwifery services program.

"What can I say, the camera loves me. In fact, I've been offered quite a few interviews. I'm going to cherry-pick the best ones to plug our midwifery program. You know I love my birth-choice soapbox." She grinned.

"Just make sure you coordinate with media relations first," Cathy said, as impervious to Mabel's cheerfulness as always.

"The line of communication is already open. We're getting overrun with new-patient requests upstairs, by the way. Sure would help to have another midwifery unit to refer them to."

Mabel raised her eyebrows in comic suggestion, and Cathy cracked a tiny smile.

"It'd be much easier if you could just clone yourself."

"I only deliver babies, not full-grown adults."

They exchanged parting waves, then continued in opposite directions down the hall. As soon as her back was turned Mabel dropped her pleasing-the-boss smile and scowled in frustration. Hospital administrators had no problem dropping millions on some razzle-dazzle digital recordkeeping system that no one could ever get to work, but hiring a couple of midwives to handle low-risk pregnancies was like convening the United Nations.

She had her suspicions as to why, and they were all ugly. But this was the framework in which she found herself, and since she had approximately zero chance of restructuring the financial decision-making in a regional hospital system, she'd just have to find a way to work through it.

She shook off the encounter as she took the elevator up to the maternity ward, where she greeted the receptionist and asked about Ashley and her newborn son.

"Of course, your hardware-store baby! Good thing you came when you did—they'll probably be discharged this afternoon. Another no-muss, no-fuss midwife delivery."

"All in a day's work," Mabel preened. The receptionist gave her the room number and she set off down the hall. She stopped to talk shop with a couple of the nurses she encountered and then rounded the corner, tossing back a joke over her shoulder.

Which is why she walked headfirst into Sam Strauss.

SAM ROCKED BACK on his heels at the impact, nearly dropping the bouquet draped over his arm as his hands rose instinctively to steady himself—and suddenly he was clutching Mabel Antonoff against his chest.

In that first instant their eyes met, her expression was wide open, and it was like looking in a mirror. She liked the way this felt, too. The warmth, the solidity, the way their bodies seemed to remember how to fit perfectly together, contour for contour, soft bulge for rock-hard—

"Watch where you're going." She jerked out of his grasp, a steel wall of irritation slamming down to sever their connection.

"Says the woman walking forward and looking backward."

"What are you doing here?" she demanded, ignoring his rather salient point.

"I came to visit Ashley and the baby."

Her eyes narrowed. "I thought you didn't want to get involved."

He didn't. But last night he'd slept terribly, unable to escape recurring, bewildering dreams about children he'd never had, the house he'd never bought, and the wife he'd never married who bore an uncanny resemblance to the woman in front of him. He'd woken up disconcerted and off-kilter, in dire need of some kind of human connection.

Plus he was hoping he'd get to hold the baby.

"I don't want to get involved in your publicity merry-go-round. Doesn't mean I want to forget what happened. It's a pretty cool experience, bringing a baby into the world."

She softened at that. "I'll give you that. Come on, then. We'll go together."

"I can wait," he offered, suddenly less enthusiastic about his errand if it involved close proximity to Mabel, but she stepped around him and rapped lightly on Ashley's door.

Ashley's husband opened it—Sam had subsequently learned his name was Luke, thanks to the chyron on the evening news—and his face split into a huge grin when he saw them.

"My favorite people! Come in. Sawyer just woke up."

Sam shuffled in behind Mabel, nodding an awkward greeting as she rushed forward to where Ashley sat in a chair, a tiny baby blinking on her shoulder.

The two women quickly became involved in a discussion peppered with mysterious terms like *lactation*, *placenta*, and *perineum*. Ashley said something about stitches and Sam turned abruptly to Luke and thrust the bouquet at him.

"Here," he said gruffly, and then hastily added, "Congratulations."

"Thanks a lot, man. These are great." Luke slapped him on the back, the glow of new fatherhood thankfully making him impervious to Sam's social incompetence.

When had he become so bad at this? His professional

success had been twenty percent strategic acumen, eighty percent charm. He'd defused hostile situations, talked roomfuls of wealthy donors out of their not-so-hard-earned cash, and literally negotiated with terrorists. Now his cheeks burned with embarrassment, he couldn't stop shifting his weight, and despite having the easiest topic of conversation imaginable fussing in its mother's arms a few feet away, he had absolutely no idea what to say.

To some extent the accident had made him lose his confidence, but that wasn't it—not entirely. Scrolling through his phone in the emergency room, scanning hundreds of contacts but not one person he knew well enough to ask to come help him, he'd realized that after a lifetime of being and doing what everyone around him wanted, he had nothing to call his own.

He'd been a dutiful child, following his overachieving older brother's lead, treading on eggshells, eager to make his parents happy, terrified to disrupt their periods of tenuous accord. He'd excelled in school and out—class president, National Honor Society, state-champion swimmer—and apart from his relationship with Mabel, he'd never once disappointed them. When he got to college he focused even more on external markers of success, like grades and accolades and job offers, investing less and less time in what fragments of a social life he still had. Ruthlessly he pushed away the dangerous openness that had previously made him a trusted friend and committed boyfriend, refusing to invest in anyone who didn't directly contribute to his academic and professional goals.

Ironic given his career was all about helping as many people as possible. But by that point the only person he'd ever really cared about was out of his life for good. He didn't deserve anyone else.

The woman in question glanced at him, her smile soft and placid as she cradled the baby against her chest. His answering smile was automatic, and long-forgotten warmth bloomed in his heart—until he realized he'd been lost in his thoughts and had no idea what, if anything, Luke had been saying to him.

Thankfully Luke had filled the gap, oblivious to Sam's mental absence as he chatted happily about Sawyer's weight, his head circumference, and his numerous and varied noises.

Sam felt cheesy as hell, but he couldn't ignore the pang of longing as Mabel gazed contentedly into the baby's face. In the years leading up to that final night, this is how he'd pictured his future—married to Mabel, having their own little family. The rest was incidental.

He watched her now, across the room, across the decade of time and disparate experiences that yawned between them.

If he could do it all again, maybe he'd choose differently.

But that's not how this worked.

"Do you want to hold him?" Ashley asked, and after a second's delay Sam realized she was talking to him.

"Yes, please," he said promptly. He was a sucker for babies.

Sam preemptively took a space on the love seat beneath the window. The doctor insisted his leg was fully healed, but he still didn't trust it not to give out on him.

Mabel squeezed in beside him, her vanilla-and-tangerine scent tangling with the unique, powdery newborn smell of the baby she held. She passed him over carefully, and Sam tucked the little man in the crook of his arm.

"Hello, *habibi*," he murmured, smiling at the tiny, irritated face looking up at him.

The baby was implausibly light beneath his hands. How could a brand-new life, with all its potential and untold magnitude, weigh less than a bowling ball?

"He's cute, huh?" Mabel asked.

"Very."

He gazed at the newborn for another minute, and then Sawyer decided he'd had enough. Mabel took the grumpy, not-quite-crying baby and passed him back to his mom, and Sam rose stiffly from the low, hard love seat.

"We should get going, but it was great to see you two. You three," Mabel amended.

"Thanks for stopping by, and for the gifts. How are you two coping with all the publicity?"

Sam glanced at Mabel for guidance; she shrugged casually, never losing her smile.

"I've always loved being the center of attention. We've even decided to do a couple of interviews together. The first one is tomorrow."

Sam groaned inwardly. Since when?

"Do you ever watch *Under the Arch*?" Mabel asked, not looking at him.

"All the time!" Ashley exclaimed, although Luke looked blank.

"Well, be sure to catch it tomorrow. You might just see some familiar faces."

They said their goodbyes to Ashley, Luke, and Sawyer. As if by tacit agreement they walked in silence down the hall and around the corner, safely away from the family's room, and then stopped in unison.

Sam opened his mouth to speak, but Mabel raised her palms.

"I know what you're going to say. I didn't tell you before now because I only accepted the invitation half an hour ago. The confirmation came through on my phone while we were with Ashley and Luke."

He was still in the mood to argue, to accuse her of foisting this on him, and ideally to talk his way out of it—but with one look at Mabel's determined expression he decided anything other than agreement would be pointless.

"Fine," he acquiesced irritably. "What is this show, anyway? I've never heard of it."

"Then clearly you've never been in any gynecologist's waiting room anywhere in the greater St. Louis area."

"You've got me there."

"It's a local, lunchtime lifestyle show that repeats again at three o'clock—after the school pickup. I wouldn't say their viewership is one hundred percent moms or caregivers… But it might be ninety-nine."

"So lots of potential midwifery clients."

She winked. "There's that honor-roll student I used to know."

"Anything in particular you want me to prepare?"

"I might text you tonight once I've had a chance to think it all through, but for the most part, I'll do the talking. Just follow my lead."

"Got it." He took a step into the center of the hallway, preparing to leave.

"Actually, there's one more thing you should know, in case it comes up." Mabel winced. "I'm divorced."

He fought so hard to keep his expression neutral that his back teeth ground together. In truth it seemed like the earth had shuddered and sighed beneath his feet—and he had absolutely no business feeling that way.

"Really," he said, impressed at how nonchalant he sounded. "Sorry to hear that."

"It's fine. We finalized it six months ago, so I've already been divorced for a quarter of the time I was married."

"Who is he?" Sam asked, veering from abject disgust at this utter moron who'd thrown away the best woman in the world to the discomfiting realization that he'd done exactly the same thing.

"No one you know. He's from Des Moines, went to Missouri State, moved out here for work. We met on an app." She rolled her eyes.

"Well," he said slowly, casting around for something to say, the distance between them widening as he processed just how much of her life he'd missed. "At least you figured it out quickly. Imagine if my parents had gotten divorced after two years."

"You wouldn't be alive," she pointed out. "Anyway, it wasn't so much a question of figuring it out as coming home to a half-empty apartment and finding a note to say he was moving to Atlanta with his ex-girlfriend—the ex-girlfriend he'd been cheating on me with for three months."

Instinctively his hands clenched into fists, and then he forced them loose. Who was he kidding? Hell yes he'd happily batter the guy if Mabel asked, but she never would. He hadn't protected her in a long time, and she didn't need him to start now.

"I'm over it, really," she assured him. "We rushed into the marriage. I should've known it would never work. Plus, he snored like a freight train."

He saw straight through her attempt at humor, but he quirked a smile, trying to follow where she led.

"So you don't want me to take out a hit on him?"

"I wouldn't go that far."

"I'll make some calls."

"You do that. And I'll see you tomorrow."

"You will," he promised.

She hesitated, a faint smile lingering on her lips, as if she couldn't decide whether or not to say something else. Then she turned abruptly, gave him a cheery wave, and strode off down the hall.

He stood a moment longer, watching her leave, her step bouncy and brisk and easy. Purposeful and unburdened.

Or at least that's what she wanted everyone to see.

He inhaled, bracing himself for the next twenty-four hours. He'd need to get his hair cut. Find something decent to wear. Look up this TV show on the Internet so he had a remote idea of how to act and what to say.

And then let the entire world know that he and Mabel Antonoff were back on speaking terms.

Chapter Five

MABEL GAPED WIDE-EYED at her reflection in the mirror, fighting the temptation to reach up and touch her lashes, which were so thickly coated with mascara that blinking required conscious effort.

"She's put way too much on my eyes. And this lipstick is so dark. I look like a vampire. Do you think I should ask her to fix it? What time is it?"

"Too late to redo your makeup. Which looks perfect, by the way."

Mabel scowled across the green room at Sam, recalling the approving once-over the makeup artist had given him when he sat in her chair. His ten-second session had involved a single application of powder, whereas she'd had two stylists hovering over her for an hour, squinting and dabbing and frowning at their palettes.

Not that she could blame them. Sam had appeared that morning with a fresh haircut, and the combination of the trim sides and loose, lazy curls spilling over his forehead made him look better suited to a magazine cover than a local, daytime TV show. His long-legged, broad-shouldered swimmer's body could turn a potato sack into a high-fashion outfit, and today's choice of dark-gray slacks and a baby-blue knit top was literally mouth-watering.

If she didn't already know that his sex appeal had always been completely effortless and unwitting, she might resent him for nabbing the spotlight. Because there was no way any viewers who were attracted to men would be listening to a word she said while he was on screen.

She sighed, turning back to the mirror. Well, she was always eager to encourage more queer and nonbinary people to try midwifery services. Maybe this was her big chance.

"The good news is that if we're randomly struck by a hurricane, my hair will still look stylish. I think someone might have swapped her hairspray for a can of industrial-strength glue." She touched the bottom of her bob, which curled stiffly toward her face.

"Quit stressing. You'll be great. No need to be nervous."

Her gaze snapped back to Sam, who hadn't even looked up from his book. Did he know that he'd basically just read her mind? That she was externally fixating on her makeup in an attempt to distract herself from the anxiety throbbing in her temples? Or was it just a lucky guess?

Mabel exhaled, crossing the room and flopping on the couch beside him. Of course it wasn't a guess. He was still as annoyingly perceptive as he'd always been.

"You aren't worried at all? Because I feel like I could quite happily throw up all over this beautifully appointed room."

He lifted a shoulder, sliding a bookmark into the thick hardcover. "Can't say I'm thrilled to be here, but I'm here nonetheless. Best I can do is stay calm and hope for a good outcome."

"What would you consider a good outcome?"

"One of the producers walking in right now to say they want to interview you by yourself, and I can go home."

At her chiding look he continued, "Failing that, you're such a roaring success that the host loses all interest in me and when we leave the studio you're mobbed by a crowd of pregnant people who make K-pop fans seem like slackers."

He bared his teeth in an exaggeratedly insincere smile and she burst out laughing. For someone who'd made it clear he didn't want to do this—multiple times over text last night, plus several in-person remarks this morning—he was maintaining a decent sense of humor.

"Thanks for being here. I know there's not really anything in it for you."

She dared to look at him squarely, something they'd both been avoiding since the start of this awkward, unexpected reunion. Emotionally she was doing her best to hold him at arm's length, and to leave the mental shoebox where she stored her memories of their relationship taped firmly shut.

But whenever she looked into his eyes, her control slipped. They were the most incredible color, an inextricable tangle of blue and gray and a hint of green that looked exactly like the ocean during a storm—or what she imagined it would look like, anyway.

Once that sea had welcomed her, its wrath a weapon for her protection as she slipped beneath the waves, floating safe and free. After he left she imagined it turning cold, icy water pushing her to shore so she was left shivering on the beach, abandoned and alone.

As their eyes met across the short space she saw that storm-churned ocean again, only now it was unfamiliar, unknowable. She couldn't trust it—but she wanted to.

"Like you said. I owe you. Plus I've always been a sucker for a noble cause."

She didn't miss the flick of his gaze to her lips, or the subtle tension in his jaw, or the telltale way he shifted in his seat.

Good God, this back-from-the-dead version of Sam Strauss wanted to kiss her.

And she…kind of wanted to kiss him, too.

Which is why she'd never been more relieved to hear the obnoxious air-horn notification sound on her phone.

She bolted up from the love seat and snatched up her phone, hastily opening her settings.

"I need to disable this stupid thing. I put it on there myself—I thought it was funny. Now it resets itself as default every time I update the app."

"Which one?" he asked, his voice a little gruff, a reminder of how close they'd just come to the unthinkable.

That's precisely what it was—unthinkable. Irrational, impossible, potentially catastrophic. She'd loved Sam once, and he'd left her. Nothing would change that, and she was pretty sure that nothing could've changed him, either. She wouldn't let him hurt her again.

She'd never let *anyone* hurt her again.

"A dating app." She smirked self-effacingly, resuming her seat beside him. "I've been a frequent flyer on these bad boys since my divorce went through."

The D-word wanted to stick in her throat, that hideous, jagged evidence of her failure, but she wouldn't let it. She wouldn't hide who she was, either, or protect him from however he might feel about the fact she'd lived more than a decade of relationships without him.

Mabel inched closer to show him the screen, steeling herself against the palpable warmth of his big body. "I've become a pretty hot commodity since our little viral splash, but it's fair to say most of these guys aren't here for the right reasons."

He frowned as he scrolled through messages ranging from blandly impersonal to downright pornographic. "How do you actually meet anyone on this thing?"

"You've never been on a dating app?"

He shook his head.

"Liar."

"I haven't, honestly."

"Then how do you find people to go out with?"

"I don't."

Her disbelief must have shown on her face because he quickly added, "I'm not celibate or anything, just busy. Some years I averaged two hundred days out of the country. Not that I'm looking for a commitment either way."

"Still don't want to be in a relationship, huh?"

"Actually, yes."

After twelve long years, she finally gave that the eye roll it deserved.

"Look at my parents' divorce," he insisted defensively. "Thirty years of hell, then they decide to go their separate ways and life is good, just like that." He snapped his fingers.

"That's only one example."

"The one most pertinent to my life."

She held up her hands. "I'm not trying to change your mind, simply stating fact. Anyway, I guess I'll take it as a compliment that you really meant it when we broke up, and it wasn't just a convenient excuse you came up with on the spot."

"Of course I meant it," he insisted, sounding mildly offended. "Trust me, I wouldn't have put us both through all of that on a whim."

"Or because you thought you might find someone better than me in college so you wanted to be single when you got there?"

He had the audacity to look wounded. "Is that what you

think? That I'd sit up all night arguing with my parents, being threatened with everything from canceling my tuition payments to kicking me out of the house, so the next day I could dump you and go play the freshman field?"

"I didn't know that about your parents," she said softly, instantly chastened as the vision of Evelyn Strauss spending hours hurling abuse at him rose all too readily to her imagination.

"My mom didn't speak to me for a month. Not one word. She didn't even say goodbye when my dad and I left to drive to school." He quirked a bitter smile. "Although I'd be lying if I said I didn't enjoy the quiet."

Mabel sighed. "Okay, I can see that in your particular context, lifelong vows to love and honor haven't yielded the best results. I'm also happier out of my marriage than I was in it, but I still believe in happily-ever-after. I am adjusting my strategy, however."

"How so?"

"I'm adopting a passive approach. Instead of pursuing men who almost always end up leaving me, I'm going to sit back and wait for Mr. Right to come my way."

Sam arched a brow, but before he could comment on her plan a sharp rap sounded on the door and one of the show's producers leaned in, smiling over the top of her clipboard.

"We're ready for you."

Mabel sucked in the biggest breath she could and held it, willing her suddenly galloping heartbeat to resume something approximating a normal rhythm. Her skin flushed and prickled at the revelation she was about to appear on television, and she was sure her ears must be the color of ripe tomatoes. Sam stood up beside her, pressing his knuckles into his lower back, and she watched him in wonderment, convinced there was no way her legs wouldn't wobble and buckle if she tried to do the same.

Then he held out his hand. She took it, and he tugged her to her feet.

She stood, steady and strong.

Get a grip, she scolded herself harshly, snatching back her hand. For twelve years Sam had been the villain in all of her nightmares, and for good reason. He was far too easy to fall for, and almost impossible to get over.

But she'd done her work, weathered the heartache, and come back stronger—for the most part. Just because life had thrown him in her path didn't mean she had to stumble all over again.

Mabel preceded Sam briskly down the hall, silently rehearsing her talking points and trying to relax her face into something smiley and easygoing. She'd always been good at public speaking, and this show didn't even have a studio audience, just the host and the production team. She could do this.

"I can do this," she whispered to herself, her nerves lifting into excitement as the producer guided them into the studio and onto two tall chairs.

Mabel blinked into the bright lights, and before she could get a good look around the set the host arrived and took her own seat across from them.

Kendra Price was a former meteorologist whose social-media expansion into makeup tutorials and family-mealtime hacks had rapidly overshadowed her ability to predict the weather. Now a local lifestyle icon, *Under the Arch* was a live, daily mix of upbeat news items, low-key guest appearances, and Kendra's own unique blend of cooking, style, and parenting how-tos.

They made their introductions, and Kendra gave them an overview of what she planned to talk about. Then she signaled to someone with a clipboard, and the next thing Mabel knew, the cameras were rolling and they were live on air.

"With me now are two people you probably know from their hashtags. Mabel Antonoff and Sam Strauss are Orchard Hill natives who joined forces to deliver a baby in a hardware store earlier this week, but these two aren't simply Good Samaritan strangers. You go way back, is that right?"

"We've known each other our whole lives," Mabel replied, pitching her tone to be cheerful and sunny. "We dated in high school, but we lost touch after graduation, so that moment in the hardware store was the first time we'd seen each other in twelve years."

"Wow. And, Sam, I hear you spent most of those twelve years in war zones."

He nodded. "I lead operations for a refugee agency, and most of my work is in the field. That's why I tried to help when I overheard a woman in labor—it wasn't the first time I'd seen a baby born outside a hospital. First time in a bathroom aisle, though," he added with a charming smile.

"Thankfully you had a midwife on hand this time. Mabel, you've been delivering little St. Louisans for years. What prompted you to choose this path?"

Mabel sat up straight, ready to grab her fifteen minutes of fame by the horns and refuse to let go.

"Funnily enough, when I started college, I wanted to be a neurosurgeon."

Mabel told the story she'd carefully devised, leaving out that she hadn't become a doctor because there was no way she'd ever be able to pay for medical school, focusing instead on midwifery's inclusivity and flexibility, and her firm belief that everyone who gives birth should have a wide range of choice, information, and control over their experience.

She felt breathless and flushed when she finished talking, but she could tell from Kendra's earnest, approving expression that she'd done well.

More importantly, she'd done exactly what she'd set out to do.

Kendra asked a couple of follow-up questions that gave Mabel a chance to plug her hospital's midwifery practice, and then she turned back to Sam.

"Thank you both for being here, and before I let you go,

I have to ask—any truth to the rumors of a romantic reconciliation?"

She glanced at Sam, who was shaking his head. Last night they'd agreed over text that the answer to this question would be no, but not so unequivocally that it didn't keep people asking. She'd read a lot of discontent in Sam's one-word replies, and now she watched him carefully.

He'd better keep his end of the bargain.

"We had something special back in the day, but I made the mistake of breaking it off and letting this one go. Mabel was just showing me her dating app right before we came out here—the competition for this woman is fierce. I don't stand a chance."

Kendra raised her brows. "You've got quite the list of suitors, huh?"

Belatedly Mabel realized she'd been gaping at Sam, her jaw hanging halfway down her neck. Had he just taken responsibility for their breakup on national—okay, *local*—television? And thrown in a wistful hint of potential pursuit, too. She couldn't have scripted such a perfect response if she'd spent a week working on it.

Unless he actually meant it?

No. No way. Not a snowball's chance in hell. And even if he did—nope. Not even going there. Not now, not ever.

"Let's just say I'm feeling popular," Mabel replied coyly.

"Good for you," Kendra enthused, and then turned to the camera. "Thanks again to my guests, our hometown heroes Mabel Antonoff and Sam Strauss. Coming up next, how to beat the September slump with some fun, healthy ideas to freshen up your kids' lunch boxes."

One of the producers announced they were clear, and Kendra slid off her seat as a makeup artist hurried over, brush already in hand.

"Great job, guys. Did you have fun?"

Mabel nodded eagerly. "This was awesome, thank you so much for having us."

"Thank you both for all the work you do for the world around us! You two have servant hearts. Maybe they'll find their way back to each other one day."

Kendra followed up her pronouncement with a wink Mabel didn't understand, and then she and Sam were being guided back to the green room, and it was too late to ask.

"You were both fantastic, really super. Just hang tight for two seconds and I'll grab your goodie bags. Again, great job!" The producer gave them a double thumbs-up, and then hurried down the hallway.

"Keep my goodie bag. I have to go." Sam flashed the kind of tight smile she'd seen on expectant mothers more times than she could count.

"What hurts?"

"Nothing."

She propped her hands on her hips, her instincts as a health practitioner momentarily overwhelming her mixed feelings about this man.

"Just tell me. Maybe I can help."

He took an interest in the blank wall beside him as he said, "A few months ago I got hit by a car while I was riding my bike in DC. That's why I took a leave of absence from work. I broke my leg, hurt my back. Supposedly it's all fine now, but I get aches sometimes."

Her heart softened, and so did her posture. She was still sort of mad at him for leaving her—well, just a little bit—but she hated the idea of him being hurt. And to think it could've been serious, that he could've—

Then again, he'd spent the better part of the last decade in places where he could've been killed at any moment, and she would've never known.

But he was here, and so was she, and she put that uneasy thought away, focusing instead on the real-life person in front of her.

"Did you do all the rehab they told you to?"

She took his *hmph* to be a no.

"I told you I know a good physical therapist. I'll ask her if there's anything she recommends."

"If it's no trouble," he said stiffly.

"Of course not." She smiled, a long-buried memory floating to the surface of her thoughts. "Were you riding with your hands in your pockets?"

He met her eyes then, and she knew he saw it as clearly as she did, his summer-long quest to perfect the ability to cycle without holding the handlebars. He'd said it was so he could keep his hands warm in his pockets in the winter, but she knew he just thought it looked cool.

Sam shook his head. "I was steering with both hands. Thought I had everything under control."

A lot went unsaid in the beat of silence that followed. Mabel felt the space between them shrinking, warming, still too big to ignore, but not quite as impassable as it once seemed.

Did that make her weak? Did generosity toward Sam mean she was selling out her own pain? She wasn't sure she was ready to forgive him—she might never be—but she didn't hate him, either.

He'd been her best friend long before he became her lover. Did the latter *have* to cost her the former forever? Or was that level of betrayal too damaging to ever let anything grow in its wake?

She had no idea. But she was about to have an *Under the Arch* tote bag, if the approaching producer's big grin was any indication.

"Sorry about that, someone moved these and it took me forever to find them. Here you go, and thanks again for joining us."

She and Sam accepted their tote bags and followed the producer out through the security gate to the parking lot. She bid them goodbye and Mabel snatched her keys from her bag, ready to get away from this situation.

"You'll let me know about the next thing, right?" Sam

asked, pulling his own keys from his pocket.

"I'm narrowing it down, but I should know soon."

"Cool. Have a good afternoon."

"You, too."

He turned, and she knew she should let him go. Let him walk away. Leave this exactly where it was.

Instead she called, "Sam?"

He glanced over his shoulder.

"Thanks for doing this today. You were great."

He smiled, and it was dazzling. "You, too. See you later."

She raised her hand in a wave, and he continued toward his car. Mabel exhaled, pivoted, and set off in the opposite direction.

She couldn't decide whether she was elated, worried, incredulous, or content, and as she caught sight of her still heavily made-up reflection in one of the building's mirrored glass windows, she stopped short.

"We've got a lot to process," she told herself.

And a lot of lipstick to wipe off and a big glass of wine to drink before she got anywhere near the topic of her gnarled, thorny feelings about her unforgettable, unforgivable, unavoidable ex-boyfriend.

Chapter Six

H E SHOULDN'T BE here.

In fact, he might leave. Randomly turning up on Mabel's doorstep was easily one of the worst ideas he'd had in a long time.

She might not be home anyway. It was Saturday night. She was probably on a date.

Sam leaned over far enough to see that a light was definitely on inside the apartment, then jerked back out of sight. The sudden movement made the floorboards creak and he froze, deciding the one thing Mabel would appreciate less than his uninvited arrival was to find him skulking outside her apartment.

She didn't appear—but her downstairs neighbor did. Mabel lived on the upper story of one of Orchard Hill's characteristic hundred-year-old houses, while the original owner remained downstairs.

Well, maybe she wasn't the *original* owner, but she couldn't be far off. Mrs. Berger had been old his whole life, a stalwart and perpetually disapproving presence at every Friday-night service at Temple Sinai. He couldn't decide whether her status as Mabel's landlord was hilarious or horrifying, given Mrs. Berger's freely offered opinion on unmarried career women in general and Norma Antonoff in particular.

He heard her scuffling around beneath the balcony where he stood, the clink of something tossed in the trash can, and then the door squeaking shut.

His shoulders eased momentarily, then stiffened again when he realized his primary problem remained unsolved.

He was still standing in front of Mabel's door.

He'd go, he decided. He'd only come here because…he wasn't sure exactly why. He'd been rooting through an old box of documents and came upon their senior prom photos, the ones where they'd stood at opposite ends of their group of friends because they'd lied about going together. He'd remembered all the times he'd fled his house after his brother's departure for college made the stifling atmosphere even more unbearable, biking the short distance to the flower shop and the girl who lived upstairs. His parents paid for his cell phone so he and Mabel devised a missed-call system, cutting the call after one ring so it wouldn't appear on the bill. He could hear it like it happened yesterday, the single, digital ring echoing in the silent alley, his hand poised over the button to—

Mabel's door swung open.

Suddenly he was face-to-face with Norma Antonoff.

"Sam?" she asked, blinking at him like someone emerging from a dream.

She'd aged gracefully, her shoulder-length hair more gray than black, her face more lined but still angularly beautiful. His mom would hate to see how good she looked, and the thought made him smile.

"Hi, Mrs. Antonoff. It's been a while."

"Yes, it has."

He watched her expression move through a range of emotions, only some of which he could identify. He set his shoulders, let her look her fill, and braced himself for whatever came next.

He had no idea how it'd all played out that night years ago, after his dad brought Mabel home. Had the two former lovers finally broken decades of tension, hurling insults in the empty street outside the flower shop? Did Norma usher her daughter inside in cold silence, saving her tirade for the privacy of their apartment? Or had she barely spared a glance for her high-school ex-boyfriend, consoling Mabel where she stood, understanding better than anyone how it felt to have the best thing in your life snatched away?

Out of their three parents, Norma had always been the most understanding, more prone to a disapproving cluck of the tongue than the all-out fury his own mother preferred.

At the same time, if he was finally confronting the man who'd broken his daughter's heart, he doubted forgiveness would be his first response.

"Well, we're here now," she murmured eventually, seemingly to herself. Then her gaze sharpened, meeting his.

"I know you were young, but you really messed up. Do you understand that?"

"Yes. If I could change it, I would."

"You can't—but maybe you can fix it."

He frowned. "How?"

"That's not up to me. But it's almost the New Year. Good time to start over."

Norma tilted her head, her expression softening. She reached up and touched his cheek briefly, the gentle, affectionate sweep of a mother's fingers.

"You were sweet kids. Both of you. Sorry we all made it so hard for you."

Sam gaped at Norma as she stepped around him.

Had she just apologized?

All those years, the effort to stay apart only to be drawn together again, feeling guilty for feeling happy, the lying, the secrecy, the awful, painful end—and she was sorry.

Just like that.

He watched her mount the top of the wooden steps that led to the ground below, reaching deep for the righteous indignation and white-hot anger this moment should inspire. The three of them had all but ruined his and Mabel's lives, adults who should've known better, who were too petty and vindictive to bury their hurt and move on, choosing instead to visit it on their unsuspecting, undeserving children.

He had every right to be furious.

But he wasn't.

Norma was right. The New Year was around the corner, with Yom Kippur hot on its heels. He didn't want to walk through this holy period full of pointless resentment and rage. He was trying to reboot his life, and forgiveness seemed like a decent way to start.

On that note, he turned back to Mabel's door. He was here, and he might as well—

"Sam?"

Norma had stopped on the top step. She hesitated, the shadows erasing decades, the edges of her mouth curling wistfully.

"How's your dad?"

"Divorced."

Her eyes widened, but she said nothing more. Just nodded goodbye and continued down the steps, out of sight.

Sam exhaled, raised his hand, and rapped on Mabel's door before he could change his mind. Again.

She answered quickly, her chin popping up as she adjusted her line of sight, having clearly expected her diminutive mother and discovering a six-foot-something man instead.

"Sam. Hi."

"Hey. I was just, um." He gestured meaninglessly to the street behind him, struggling to form a coherent thought now that he'd seen the snug, ribbed, light-blue tank top she wore—and realized that she wasn't wearing a bra underneath.

"You mentioned some exercises," he said finally. "I thought maybe you could show me."

"Is your phone broken?"

"No, why?"

"Because you could've called instead of showing up at my house, unannounced, at eight o'clock on a Saturday night."

She had him there. "If you're busy—"

"I'm not. Come in. I had a hunch you were coming anyway."

"Really?" He followed her through the front door.

She shot him a bemused look over her shoulder as she led him into what had once probably been a large bedroom, or even two knocked together, which now served as her living room.

"Did you seriously think you could ask Josh for my address and he wouldn't tell me? Sit."

He dropped onto the couch, which was soft and worn and remarkably comfortable. The whole room was Mabel to a T—colorful, inviting, cluttered, and a little disorganized. An enormous houseplant sprawled in one corner, the bookshelf bordered on overflowing, a jasmine-scented candle burned on the windowsill, and a veritable rainbow of artwork crammed the walls. The space was homey and comfortable in a way he'd been missing at his grandmother's empty, echoing house, and he relaxed instantly, already feeling better about his decision to come.

Whether Mabel agreed was a different matter.

She propped her hand on her hip, her attempt to seem put out undermined by the intrigued twinkle in her eyes. "I presume you want something to drink. I've got beer, wine…"

"You can't want to get rid of me that badly if you're trying to get me drunk."

She dropped her hand and smiled, just a little. "Actually my plan was to drug you and sell your kidney. Will that be a problem?"

"Not at all—I've got a spare. Beer, please."

"Coming right up."

He sank back into the cushion, stretching his legs in front of him. Even though their connection had grown stiff and awkward through years of absence and hurt, he had to admit that he still felt it. Something about Mabel had always been magnetic, drawing him toward her, comforted in her presence even when she was unhappy with him.

Was he wrong to indulge himself now, knowing he'd be gone soon? No, not if he was honest with her—and with himself.

Mabel returned with two cans of local brews. Instead of taking the emerald-green armchair across from the sofa she sat down beside him, extending her can to tap his.

"Cheers."

"Cheers," he echoed, and took a long, bolstering sip. She was close enough for him to see the chipped polish on her toes as she pulled her legs up beneath her, to breathe in the vanilla-and-tangerine scent that always made his heart race, to catch a glimpse of the shadowed hollow between her breasts.

He leaned forward to put his can on the coffee table, carefully arranging the coaster beneath it. When he sat up again Mabel was watching him, wearing a half smirk.

"Did Josh give you a hard time when you asked him for my address?"

"Yes. At least, I think so. I stopped reading after the fifteenth text."

"He has a lot to say."

"I'll call him tomorrow, let him get it all out. It's only fair."

She set down her own beer and then leaned back against the cushion, crossing her arms.

"What really brings you to my doorstep this evening?"

"I was going through some old paperwork and found our prom photos, and it reminded me of sneaking out to see you. I thought I'd do it again, for tradition's sake."

"Only without the subterfuge, since no one cares where you go these days."

"I suppose not," he said, reaching for his beer, hoping it would fill the uncomfortable, hollow space her words inadvertently opened in his chest.

"You know, every time I imagined what I'd say if I ever saw you again—not that I spent a ton of time thinking about you, so don't flatter yourself—I had a different but equally long and detailed speech prepared. But honestly? I'm tired of being mad at you. Maybe I'm stabbing my heartbroken teenage self in the back by saying that, but it's true. It's nice to talk to you again, see that you're okay, and didn't actually morph into the total asshole I had you down as."

"I wouldn't go that far," he joked, hoping his grin wasn't as big and goofy as it felt. That was the kindest thing anyone had said to him in months.

"It's good to see you, too," he admitted, and then extended his hand. "Friends?"

"Friends." She shook his hand firmly, and that fleeting brush of palms shouldn't have left his skin feeling scorched, shouldn't have sent heat rushing through his chest, and absolutely shouldn't have made him desperate to touch her again.

And again, and again, and again.

"I saw your mom," he told her, ready to change the subject. "Outside, as she was leaving."

Mabel's brows shot up. "And you still seem to have all your teeth. Must've gone well."

"Actually, she apologized."

"For what?" Mabel asked cautiously.

"She said, 'sorry we made it hard for you,' I think meaning the three of them and both of us."

"Wow."

Mabel took a sip and then studied the can, turning it

around in her hand.

"I'm not sure whether that makes me happy or freaking furious," she said finally.

"That's exactly what I thought."

"I guess anger isn't a constructive emotion."

"But it feels damn good sometimes," he offered, and she laughed.

"Well, she didn't say it to me, so it doesn't count. Now, tell me about this broken leg."

She must've read the surprise on his face because she added, "Don't think you can come over here pretending to want help with rehab and then not have to do it. I'm going to make you work."

He groaned inwardly, but he didn't argue.

"It was a tibia fracture here." He drew a diagonal line across his left calf, and Mabel winced.

"Can I see?"

Before he could answer she was on the floor, shoving his jeans up his leg.

He fought the urge to flinch as she ran her thumb over the red, raised scar that slashed across his shin. She whistled, gripping his ankle to follow its progress back over his calf.

"That's your friendly reminder to always look both ways before turning right on red."

His tone was playful, but when she looked up her mouth was a grim line.

"This must've been a major accident. No wonder you're

freaked out."

"I'm not freaked out," he said quickly, jerking his leg out of her grip.

"To be honest, with this scale of injury I'm impressed you're walking at all," she continued, ignoring his protest as she motioned him up. "Stand next to me."

He eyed her warily, but did as he was told.

"Now, I'm not a physical therapist, but I have some experience working with women on regaining abdominal and pelvic strength after giving birth."

"My pelvis is just fine, thank you."

"If you don't keep quiet I'll check for myself. Now, put your weight on your left foot. Can you hold that for twenty seconds?"

"Probably." He winced, less at the dull ache in his lower leg, more at the unnerving feeling of instability. He hated feeling weak, and Mabel seeing him that way made it much worse.

"That's good enough," he told her, but she grabbed his left arm to keep him in position.

"That was five seconds. Come on, show me what you got. Can you pick up your other foot?"

He exhaled irritably but did as she asked. In truth he'd been shown this exact exercise by the physical therapist in DC—the one he saw for a single session and then never went back.

His leg was firm beneath him, and the pain wasn't even

that bad, yet his cheeks were hot, his chest tight. A minute ago he'd been perfectly comfortable but now he felt overdressed, overheated, claustrophobic in the small room.

Mabel's hand was still on his arm, light and gently steadying, but the more he thought about it, her touch, her proximity, the simple fact of being here with her, the more wobbly he became.

His ankle started to give way beneath him. He rocked onto the edge of his foot, trying to stop the inevitable, but it was too late.

He was losing this fight with gravity, and he was taking Mabel with him.

In the instant before they hit the ground Sam caught Mabel by the waist and shifted so he didn't land on top of her, taking the brunt of the impact on his side and hip instead. The air rushed out of his lungs on a muttered expletive as they hit the floor. His arm was caught under her and he tugged it out, leaving him propped up on his elbows, Mabel flat on her back beneath him.

Mabel stared up at him, her dark eyes round with surprise, squeezing his upper arms like she hadn't quite realized they'd landed. His knee was between her legs, their stomachs pressed together, faces just inches apart.

He should move. Roll off and apologize. Help her to her feet with a chaste hand, and then get the hell out of here before he did something stupid.

Another something stupid, to be accurate.

But then she stirred beneath him, lifting her hand to sweep the hair off his forehead. Her fingers trailed down the side of his face, and then drifted to the back of his neck, urging him closer.

"Mabel," he cautioned, but she shook her head. She put her index finger to her lips, and then to his, her own tongue peeking out to mirror the path she traced along his mouth.

"This is a terrible idea," he grumbled.

Then he kissed her.

He'd fantasized about this moment hundreds, maybe thousands of times over the last twelve years. They'd run into each other at an airport, or a restaurant, or—his personal favorite—on a secluded beach halfway around the world. A few words exchanged and the past was put right, wrongs forgotten. She'd reach for him, a little shyly. He'd cup her jaw, tilt her chin up. They'd kiss as a wave crashed against the rocks behind them. One final time together, their bodies finding easy, unspoken closure.

After that it got X-rated pretty quickly, but never mind—this was better than even the wildest, most exotic scenario he'd ever conceived.

The cheap carpet scratched his forearms, he could smell that the previous tenant had been a smoker, his hip throbbed where he'd landed on it, and life was absolutely glorious. He kissed Mabel like they'd never been apart, without self-consciousness or restraint, as if the corruptions of adulthood hadn't been allowed to interfere in their pure, youthful connection.

She was soft and warm beneath him, no longer the girl he'd known but not altogether different, either. She tasted the same, but richer. Her body curved more lusciously against his, supple and round and soft. Her mouth moved with confidence, not bashfulness, widening and sucking, her tongue finding his with surety and self-possession.

Mabel was a woman now, and had been for a long time. Not the inexperienced teen on the brink of maturity, but a master of her sexuality, an agent of her own desire.

She may have loved me first, but she loved others better.

A thought so ugly and unbidden that he physically recoiled, withdrawing from her as suddenly as if her ex-husband had marched into the room and pushed him off.

She sat upright as he eased away, propping his back against the couch.

"What happened?" she asked, breathless and bewildered.

"Good question."

He ran his hands through his hair, trying to align his muddled, resistant head with his desperate, yearning body. Clearly Mabel was open to this…whatever it was, and a big part of him wanted it, too.

But an even bigger part insisted she could do better, and he would only be wasting her time.

"Things between us are complicated enough already. We probably shouldn't make it worse," he told her with an apologetic smile.

"I guess not," she agreed, sounding reluctant.

"I won't be in town much longer, and you've got your whole dating-app situation. Strike while the iron's hot," he offered feebly, trying to not to cringe at his own flimsy effort to justify a decision he wasn't wholeheartedly on board with.

"Plus your whole 'I don't want a relationship' business. You must be fighting off the ladies with lines like that." She quoted him in an over-the-top, stuffy-old-man voice and he had to smile.

"Certainly makes the speed-dating go faster."

"Do people still do that?"

He meant it as a joke, but she seemed to be waiting for an answer, so he shrugged. "I honestly don't know. I've basically been single my entire adult life."

"Single… But not celibate?"

Heat suffused his face, and he knew his ears were red. "No, not celibate."

"Can't say I ever figured you for the one-night-stand type."

"Guess you don't know me as well as you thought you did."

What was intended to be a lighthearted comment thudded between them like a brick. He'd stretched their tentative familiarity and now it threatened to snap, flinging them back on opposite sides of the divide.

"It's easier that way, more honest," he continued, snatching at the swiftly retreating shreds of their accord. "I don't want to mislead anyone. When both parties are fully committed to not committing, it works just fine."

"I'll have to take your word for it." She popped up on her knees to grab her beer. "I guess I shouldn't judge. I got dragged all the way to the altar by someone who turned out not to have a committed bone in his body."

"You'll do better. And he'll regret it."

"Do you?"

Clear and sharp, her question sliced straight through his heart. Did he regret hurting her? Of course he did, every day. Did he regret hurting her at eighteen instead of twenty-one, or twenty-five, or whenever his father's prediction came true and they finally accepted that their relationship was making them miserable? He wasn't sure—at least not as sure as he used to be.

Did he regret not being the man she deserved, then or now? Yes. Yes, he did.

"Never mind," she muttered, seeming to find some conclusion in his silence as she took a swig from her can.

"You know we've got that other interview on Tuesday," she said, bringing this heavy conversation to an abrupt close.

"I know—I got your text. I'll be there."

"What's happening with the house?"

"I've chosen a realtor. She's coming to take pictures on Monday."

"Good stuff. Anyway, it's getting late."

He nodded, the message landing loud and clear. Gingerly he pushed himself up. He'd be sore tomorrow, but he did his best to keep his movements loose and easy.

He supposed it was too late for Mabel to see him as strong and capable—but that didn't mean he wouldn't try.

"Thanks for the beer," he said as he moved toward the door.

"Thanks for the visit," she replied, and he was pretty sure she meant it.

Neither of them lingered on the doorstep, although after she shut the door behind him he bet she moved to the window, watching through the curtains to make sure his car started, even though it was a relatively new, perfectly reliable model.

That was Mabel, though. Caring, attentive, loyal to a fault.

At least, that's who she *had* been. He barely knew who she was now. He'd do well to remember that, he chided himself as he descended the steps and got into his car, which started just fine.

They were different people, he repeated silently.

Too bad her ability to thoroughly tempt, distract, and confound him hadn't changed a bit.

Chapter Seven

MABEL SLAMMED HER car door shut, pressed the button to lock it, and ran like hell—or the closest equivalent given her high-heeled shoes—across the parking lot.

Today was their biggest interview, not to mention her last chance to make the most of what remained of her fifteen minutes of fame, and of course everything was going wrong.

She wasn't scheduled to be on-call last night, but then not one, not two, but *three* of the practice's moms went into labor. She'd gotten a call shortly after midnight asking her to come in and lend a hand, and she doubted telling the harried labor-and-delivery nurse that she needed her beauty sleep before her six-a.m. live appearance on a national morning show would go down well.

The first two babies arrived swiftly and with minimal fuss—inevitably those were the births her colleague was attending—but number three decided to take a more leisurely approach. By the time mom and baby were settled she was not only running dangerously late, she was splattered in all the fluids that accompany the entrance of a brand-new life into the world.

Her plans for unrushed coffee, a healthy breakfast, and a relaxed spell in front of the mirror became a hasty, lukewarm shower in the staff room and a stale, sickly-sweet cinnamon bun from the vending machine.

At least the traffic won't be bad at this time of the morning, she'd consoled herself—and then turned into a street where cars crept at a glacial pace, bumper-to-bumper, around a tire blocking the left lane.

Finally she reached the office park where she and Sam were scheduled to use the videoconference facilities for their brief but hopefully monumental appearance on a superpopular early-morning show broadcast live from New York City. She parked her car with zero concern for the white lines demarcating the spaces, sprinted across the asphalt, and hurled herself through the front door, sweaty and disheveled and beyond stressed.

Then she realized she was in the wrong building.

She choked back a defeated sob, ready to cancel the whole damn thing.

Her phone rang in her purse and she snatched it up, simultaneously hopeful and terrified that it might be the TV producer.

Sam.

"I'm trapped in a waking nightmare," she said by way of greeting.

"Good morning to you, too," he replied pleasantly. "How can I help?"

He sounded so composed, so steady, so *Sam*, and it pushed her straight over the edge.

She wasn't quite sure what she blubbered into the phone, or if he understood it any better than she did, but he knew exactly what to say to calm her down. Soon he was giving her directions to find the correct building—which wasn't as far away as she'd feared—and within minutes she was in the right place at almost the right time, with the right man waiting in the lobby.

Okay, she wouldn't go quite that far—but at the moment he felt pretty damn close.

He walked forward to meet her and although every atom in her body screamed at her to fall against him, to let him close his arms around her and hold her upright, she resisted. She'd already spent the last few nights waking up in the wee hours, tasting their ill-advised kiss from Saturday, the weight and heat of him pressed against her still echoing in her bones. She'd never been so tempted by a man—or had so many reasons to keep her distance.

But did she really? She asked herself the question for the thousandth time as he led her down the hall to the videoconference room.

Yes, he'd mishandled a bad situation at eighteen and broken her heart. But he hadn't ruined her life. She'd gotten over it—for the most part—and moved on. Dated other people. Even gotten married, and at no point during the engagement or the wedding planning or the big day itself did she sit back and think, *If this ends in divorce, it'll be Sam Strauss's fault.*

And he'd apologized. That was worth something.

He didn't want a commitment, and she didn't want anything else—not in the long run, anyway. Would a quick fling really be such a bad idea? Their physical chemistry still sizzled, and despite his definite potential to behave like one, Sam wasn't actually a jerk. The clock was ticking down to the moment she hung up her romantic running shoes and let love find her. Why not go out with one last fleeting, no-strings bang?

Her mental gears creaked as she switched them to the present. Sam opened the door and she saw that the camera was already switched on, projecting her pale, puffy face onto the huge screen on the opposite wall. They wouldn't be live for another ten minutes or so, but that version of herself needed at least an hour to look halfway decent.

"I look awful," she muttered gloomily.

"You look beautiful," Sam insisted, and she almost believed him.

Mabel heaved a sigh and hauled out her makeup bag, attempting aesthetic damage control while also trying to talk herself into a better mood. This was her big nationwide moment, and she needed to be bright and bubbly and interesting and endearing.

In other words, the exact opposite of how she felt.

"There's a producer from the show watching the feed on

the other end, but we can't see them, just the broadcast," Sam explained, and she glanced up, realizing the live show was visible on the other half of the screen. "When I got here the tech guy at the front told me to come in and sit down. Next thing I know this disembodied voice is talking to me, calling me by my name. For a second I thought it was God."

She cracked a smile. "Did you take the opportunity to ask any burning theological questions?"

"Thankfully I figured out pretty quickly that an omnipotent deity wouldn't ask me what the weather was like in St. Louis."

He was trying to make her laugh, and she could've kissed him for it. Except it would destroy her freshly applied lipstick.

And possibly her life.

That little hyperbole *did* make her chuckle. Poor, handsome Sam, sitting there patiently, totally unaware of his potential to ruin her for all other men, forever. Who knew, if that one night had gone differently, if they hadn't been caught, they might be married with kids now. He'd be stuck with her for eternity.

Her smile faltered.

Just as well, then.

"Hey, guys, we're going to have you on air shortly, okay?"

Mabel jumped as the voice of the invisible producer came through the video link.

"Got it," Sam said, then mouthed, "See?"

She gave her hair one last fluff and climbed onto one of the two stools. She adjusted her posture, folded her hands in her lap, and tried to look at anything except herself on the screen.

The voice returned, reminded them to have fun, and counted down as the audio feed from the studio simultaneously grew louder. Mabel heard her own name as one of the presenters introduced their story, and the next thing she knew she was live on TV, grinning at a famous broadcaster.

"Thank you both for joining us this morning. Walk us through what happened in the hardware store that day. One minute you're browsing, the next you're attending a birth. What was that like?" Leila Azad, a ubiquitous network favorite, smiled encouragingly.

"I still haven't gotten the towel rail I'd gone there to buy," Sam began, and Mabel relaxed slightly as he took the lead in recounting the incident, giving her a few moments to gather her thoughts before Leila turned to her.

"Mabel, you've been a practicing midwife for years. Tell me, was this the most unexpected place you've ever delivered a baby?"

"It's a close second," she answered, and briefly recounted her carefully prepared—and only slightly embellished—anecdote about the baby she'd delivered in a hotel parking lot on her honeymoon.

"My goodness," Leila replied, looking genuinely astonished, and panic shot through Mabel's chest as she wondered whether she'd gone too far. Maybe she should've stuck to the narrative that this birth was unparalleled rather than one-upping herself. But she'd thought it was a funny story, and added to the wildness and unpredictability of it all, and hopefully she'd be more memorable if—

"Sounds like your marriage got off to a dramatic start," Leila added, and it all clicked into place.

The romance, Mabel thought, mentally thwacking the heel of her hand against her forehead. She should've said vacation instead of honeymoon. Now Leila was thrown, because she'd planned to transition into the still-bubbling speculation about her and Sam's relationship status.

"That was probably its high point. I'm divorced," she said as flippantly as she could manage around her exaggerated grin.

She read the slight easing in Leila's posture at that comment.

Don't worry, we're back on track.

"Sam isn't your ex-husband, but he is your ex-boyfriend, is that right?"

"We were high-school sweethearts, but we lost touch in college," he said.

High-school sweethearts, she thought approvingly. She'd have to commend him later on that colorful turn of phrase.

"And when you met again in the hardware store, how long had it been since you'd seen each other?"

"Twelve years," they said in unison, then looked at each other, laughed, and turned back at the camera.

The moment was unchoreographed and pure luck, but Leila looked delighted, and Mabel knew they'd just scored TV gold. She fisted her hand in her lap, a triumphant thrill running up her spine.

Leila asked her about midwifery, and she gave the little spiel she'd adapted for a nationwide audience, skipping the specifics of her own practice and focusing instead on the importance of a wide range of accessible childbirth options for all pregnant people.

Leila had a couple of follow-up questions, and then continued, "We're almost out of time, but I have to ask what we're all wondering—any likelihood of a second-chance romance for you two?"

This time they'd planned the ambiguous glance they exchanged, as well as Mabel's response. "Never say never."

"Thank you both so much for being here. Up next, the Rosh Hashanah holiday is right around the corner. We'll learn how students from a Hebrew school in Maryland are helping their community get a fresh start for the Jewish New Year, right after the break."

"And we're out. Great job, guys," the bodiless producer said, and Mabel sagged with relief.

After a few parting pleasantries the feed cut altogether, and she and Sam looked at each other.

"We're done," he said with a smile, and the implications

of those two words hit her like a slate tile blown off a roof.

They weren't just done with their brief media round. This strange, unexpected interlude in which they were thrown together again was over.

"What's happening with the house?" She tried to sound casual, to conceal what felt like a sucking wound in the pit of her stomach.

"Went on the market yesterday. Apparently the realtor's already had a couple of requests for showings, so I don't think it'll take long to sell."

"Do you know when you're leaving?"

He shook his head. "I haven't booked a flight yet, but I'd like to be out of here by Yom Kippur."

"Why?"

His expression turned curious and she added, "I mean, that seems kind of arbitrary. Do you have big plans for the holiday or something?"

"No, but I can't hang around here forever. I have to get back to my life. That seems as good a deadline as any."

"So you're going back to DC?" She was stalling now, but she couldn't stop herself. For all she knew she was being foolish—she wasn't ready to let him go.

"To begin with, at least. I'm itching for my next overseas assignment, but"—he lifted a shoulder—"my manager keeps saying I need to take it easy."

"Why?"

"Is this an interrogation? Because if I'm going to be here

awhile, I'll sit down."

His tone was only half joking, and she knew she was pushing her privileges as his friend, or ex, or whatever she was. "Sorry for being interested in your life choices."

He waved his hand dismissively. "It's fine—kind of a sore spot, I guess. My boss keeps insisting that I not rush my return. I think he's worried I'm traumatized from the accident, and he doesn't want me dealing with a delayed mental-health fallout in a war zone."

"You disagree?"

"Completely. I live for the adrenaline, and the complexity, and the challenges. I get melancholy when I'm not out in the field. Downbeat. Normal life is a drag."

"Well, I hope you get your wish and are dodging bullets soon. Orchard Hill must be on the verge of murdering you with its low crime rate and well-maintained thoroughfares."

"Orchard Hill isn't all sunshine and daffodils—not for me, anyway. Everyone hates me. As I'm sure you're aware, Josh told Ellie and Saul I'm back and now all three of them are abusing my poor phone. Well, mostly Ellie and Josh. Saul sent an emoji of a middle finger and left it at that."

Mabel couldn't stifle her smile at her friends' loyalty. "They'll come around."

"I doubt it. Not that it matters—I'm probably *persona non grata* to the rest of Orchard Hill, too, the big shot who broke the girl next door's heart and then hightailed it out of town, never to be heard from again."

"No one hates you," she scoffed. "You were the golden boy. I'm the slut who tried to ruin your life."

His jaw dropped, anger flashing in his eyes. "Who said that?"

"No one worth mentioning. You remember how it was, the gossip about our parents, the stories that made your mom the victim and mine the ungrateful harlot."

She shrugged, doing her best to bat away the memories of whispers behind hands, of her mother stiffening as they walked through the grocery store, of passersby slowing to peer through the flower-shop window but never setting a foot inside.

"What happened back then had nothing to do with us."

"It shouldn't, but it did. The rumor mill cranked into action again after you left. I don't know who found out what, but the story was I'd tried to get pregnant to trap you into marrying me."

Sam scowled. "That's absurd. And disgusting. And malicious as hell. I'm sorry that happened to you, Mabel. I had no idea."

"Ancient history," she said flippantly, stuffing that old hurt back down in the darkness where it belonged. "My point is, no one hates you."

"Except our friends. And your mom."

"My mom apologized to you," she pointed out. "And Saul and Josh and Ellie will get over it, if they haven't already."

He looked skeptical, but he kept quiet, and she realized what he wasn't saying.

He'd be gone soon. Did it really matter?

"Anyway, I've been up all night. I'd better get home if I have any chance of a nap before my shift this afternoon." She stretched, easing off the stool.

They left the room together, but Sam stopped as soon as they got to the lobby, pointing his thumb over his shoulder. "I parked in the other lot."

"Oh. Okay. Well, thanks for doing this with me."

"No worries. I hope it turns you into the most successful and sought-after midwife in the Midwest."

"Sure you don't want to do a couple more? I'm still getting tons of interview requests." She raised her brows in mock hopefulness.

"No, but I'm happy to sign over my half of our story. You can tell it to whoever you want."

"Maybe," she said noncommittally, but she knew this was the end of it all.

"Will I see you at shul for Rosh Hashanah?" she asked.

She was teasing, but his answering tone was serious. "I don't think so."

"Guess this is it, then."

"It's been good to see you again. I'm glad you're doing so well."

"Likewise," she said softly.

He inclined his head, a formal, final gesture of farewell.

"Take care of yourself, Mabel."

"You, too."

She couldn't stand his awkward, hands-in-pockets posture a second longer. Mabel launched herself at Sam, flinging her arms around his neck.

At first he was stunned, stiff—and then he opened his arms and held her tightly, squeezing like he had no intention of ever letting go.

Tears threatened behind her lids and she angled her face against his chest, her nose pressed into his sternum, burying herself in his warmth and scent.

"Let's get together before I leave," he murmured, her ear so close to his neck that his voice seemed to resonate through her body. "Go out for coffee or something."

She nodded, certain it wouldn't happen, painfully confident this was the last time she'd see him before their lives diverged again. As much as she'd fantasized otherwise, she doubted she could handle anything more, no matter how short-lived and uncommitted they promised each other it would be. He'd leave, she'd be sad, and pining over another runaway man was not how she wanted to start the New Year.

Not this one, not any one, ever again.

"Whatever you end up doing, be happy. You deserve it," she told him forcefully.

She felt his hesitation and she tightened her grip, as if she could press self-belief into him. Convince him that he should let someone love him, that it wouldn't make him unhappy at all, and that he might just discover he loved her in return—whoever she was.

He eased back just enough to draw her attention, to prompt her to look up at him. She met his gaze, focused and intent, those bottomless twin oceans in his eyes clear and calm.

He wanted to kiss her. She could read his intention perfectly, because she wanted to kiss him, too.

And in one of the greatest acts of willpower she'd ever imagined, let alone achieved, she tugged herself free and took a decisive step backward.

She wouldn't say *See you later*. She wouldn't say *See you soon*. She wouldn't lie to either of them.

"Bye, Sam."

He raised his palm, then let it fall back against his side.

She turned on her heel and walked away, shoulders back, chin high.

This was exactly the closure she needed, she told herself. No more unanswered questions, no more what-ifs. Time to move on and start over.

Again.

Chapter Eight

SAM DRUMMED HIS fingers on the steering wheel, trying to enjoy this forced downtime, and hoping none of his neighbors called him in as a suspicious person loitering on the road.

The couple viewing his grandmother's house had significantly overrun their allotted time, which he guessed was a good sign. He'd parked behind the realtor's car, figuring they were almost done, but he'd been waiting nearly half an hour.

He pressed back in his chair, extending his legs as far as they'd go in the small car. Too late to change course now, and anyway, how much longer could they be? He crossed his arms over his chest and closed his eyes, tapping into his warzone-honed ability to grab a nap wherever the opportunity presented itself.

As always, the instant he shut his lids his mind buzzed with all the preoccupations and to-dos and concerns that lived just below the surface of his consciousness, and which only bubbled up in the gaps between the day's distractions. Chief among these was Mabel, followed closely by his persistent worries about his career, his future, and his imminent but still-unscheduled departure from Orchard Hill.

He sank past the latter easily, but Mabel was harder to escape. His thoughts caught on her like a branch jutting out from the side of a cliff, a tempting handhold keeping him from falling into the oblivion of sleep.

They'd said goodbye—their story was over. The whole point of this exercise was to reconnect with the best of who he'd been, and then close this chapter for good, and he'd achieved it. He had no excuse for spending the last few days still fixated on her, wondering what she was doing, if she thought about him, if he might see her again. Useless, counterproductive mental circles tugging him toward the past when his future required attention with gathering urgency.

A car door slammed somewhere down the street and Sam opened his eyes, exhaling in exasperation.

Maybe a nap wasn't on the cards after all.

He was flexing his ankle, evaluating whether his leg would be up to a time-killing walk to Main Street when his phone rang. He groaned when he read his boss's name on the display, but answered with a professional and borderline friendly "Khaled, how are you?"

"Hey, Sam, I'm good. I'm glad I caught you—have you got a second? I know the holiday starts soon."

Sam's mouth tightened. He'd been avoiding this conversation for weeks, letting Khaled's calls go to voice mail, leaving his emails unread. His boss had been sensitive and accommodating throughout Sam's recovery, but calling a couple of hours before Rosh Hashanah celebrations began at sunset meant he wanted to talk. He knew Sam would be at home or on his way, with no excuse to get him out of this discussion.

"Your timing's ideal," Sam said, amusing himself with his private irony. "I'm actually sitting in my car outside my grandmother's house, waiting for some potential buyers to leave."

"That sounds promising. It's on the market, then?"

"Already getting a lot of interest. I should be out of here soon."

"Great," Khaled said, sounding relieved. "I was hoping you'd say that. I've got an assignment coming up that I think you'll be excited about."

Sam leaned forward, his heart rate increasing. When he'd asked Khaled for a sabbatical, he'd said he needed time to recover from the accident and sort out his grandparents' property. Although Khaled had openly suggested that an accident of that severity may require mental as well as physical recovery, Sam had never revealed the extent of his self-doubt, his knocked confidence, or his genuine concern that he'd lost the ruthless focus and drive that had made him good at his job in the first place.

Now here he was, months later, feeling…a little bit better about his career. As he'd hoped, he'd slowly begun to find his way back to the adolescent passion that inspired him to choose this path in the first place. Rereading some of the school assignments his grandparents had kept, revisiting his teenage insistence on fighting for global justice, the echoes of that unshakable belief in his ability to change the world had resounded in his mind. He'd had such faith in himself, then.

And so had Mabel.

"I don't want you jumping right back into the field, so this isn't a hardship posting. In fact, it could even be described as cushy."

"Okay," Sam said cautiously.

"We're partnering on a refugee resettlement program in Europe, and one of the local agencies has asked us for someone who can help set up their service hub. They need some strategic advice on how to triage the needs of this particular refugee community—assembling immediate aid, coordinating external resources, developing in-house programs for education, job-seeking, language skills."

"But I've only ever dealt with emergency-response situations. I wouldn't know where to start," Sam told his boss, bewildered that Khaled thought this would be a good fit for him.

"Trust me, you can do this in your sleep," Khaled exclaimed on a laugh. "They've already got it ninety-percent figured out, but they want someone from our agency to troubleshoot and pat them on the back. Be a presence, give everything the seal of approval, take a couple of photos with the mayor or whoever. Who better than you? You're practically a household name these days."

Sam heard the amusement in his manager's voice and the teasing reference to his short-lived celebrity. "I guess you've seen the hashtags."

"Hashtags, video, morning TV—you've had an eventful trip back home."

"I probably should've called the press office, but I didn't realize—"

"It's fine," Khaled interjected, his tone dismissive. "It's a pretty heroic story, actually—a good look for us. Which makes you an even better candidate for this assignment. Here's the best part—guess where it's located."

Sam tried to imagine what constituted cushy in his line of work. "Lagos?"

"Helsinki."

"Finland?"

"How does that sound?"

"Cold."

Khaled laughed, but Sam wasn't joking. Rubber-stamping a well-organized resettlement operation in Helsinki sounded dull and tedious and genuinely very cold.

And maybe not the worst place for him to be.

Back in the fold, but with his foot off the professional gas, he could take advantage of the low-stress assignment to work on his goals. Assess how to build out the nonwork side of his life so he never found himself in the back of another ambulance with no one to call. He might even—gasp—make a friend.

"Can I think about it?" he asked his boss.

"You can, but not for long. They want someone yesterday, but if it's you who's coming I can probably hold them off."

"Yom Kippur is the middle of next week. Can I call you then?"

Khaled sighed, broadcasting that was longer than he wanted to wait. "At the latest. If you decide sooner, let me know."

"I will," Sam promised. They hung up and Sam shoved his phone into his pocket, and then glanced through the windshield just in time to see the realtor leaving with the potential buyers.

The couple looked young, younger than him—late twenties, maybe. They sported matching shiny-gold wedding rings, and optimistic smiles. When the woman turned in profile, he thought he could just make out the swell of early pregnancy.

He smiled, but melancholy tugged heavily on his heart. He was happy for them, hopeful they'd breathe new life into this long-empty family home, fill it once again with the clatters and stomps of growing feet. He'd give them a good deal, a boost on the ladder, if he could.

The realtor and her potential buyers left, and he hauled himself inside, challenging himself to put weight on his leg as he moved through the house. An unfamiliar perfume hung within some of the rooms, and it seemed as though the walls receded wherever he caught it, the distance between him and what had once been his grandparents' home increasing.

He wished he could be sad, sort of missed the sharp bite of grief when his grandfather died, or when his grandmother's dementia first obscured the woman he'd known all his life. That was all so long ago now, and living in their house had underlined that fact.

He wouldn't miss it. He didn't think he would miss anything in Orchard Hill, except—

"Helsinki," he said aloud, the word echoing in the empty kitchen. "Let's see what you're about."

He sat down, took out his phone, typed in *F-I-N-L*—and then changed his mind.

His time in Orchard Hill was almost over, and he had to admit the town had served him as well as he could've hoped. He'd readied the house for sale, said goodbye to Mabel, even received an unexpected apology from her mom. But he'd done it all mostly in isolation, still resisting the community connections he'd once known here.

That would be high on his agenda of life changes once he reached Helsinki. In the meantime, he owed himself one more step outside his comfort zone.

He checked the time. If he moved fast, he'd make it.

"Hey, scoot over." Ellie Bloom leaned over the edge of the already tightly packed back-row pew where Mabel sat beside her high-school friends, Hanh and Josh.

"You're dating the rabbi's son, you should be down the front," Mabel grumbled, but shifted over, letting Ellie squeeze in next to her.

"And make a spectacle of the fact I barely made it to Erev Rosh Hashanah services in time for the Oneg? No thanks."

"Girl, same," Mabel whispered, and they exchanged a conspiratorial smile.

She returned her attention to Rabbi Spellman, trying to calm her swirling, fragmented, postworkday thoughts. As usual all of her appointments ran behind schedule—one of her biggest failings according to hospital management, but when she got chatting with her patients she just couldn't help herself—and she'd rushed to Temple Sinai, where she'd found the lobby empty as everyone had already taken their seats in the sanctuary.

Her mom had taken her usual place on the left-hand side, fourth row from the front, but thankfully Mabel spotted Josh and Hanh at the back, saving her the walk of shame up to join her.

Now she looked around the room, taking silent attendance. There was her landlady, Mrs. Berger. Ellie's boyfriend, Jonah, up-front and attentive, just like any good rabbinical-school dropout should be. Behind him sat Ellie's sister, her husband, and their two boys. And behind them was—wait, wasn't that the lady who'd taken over the thrift store downtown? Mabel groped for her name, digging her teeth into her bottom lip.

"Shove over, Bloom."

Mabel glanced over at the urgent whisper, to find her high-school bestie, Saul, and his girlfriend, Eve, at the end of the pew.

"Seat's taken," Ellie said primly, folding her hands in her lap.

Saul turned imploring eyes on her. "Mabel, can you please dump Ellie on the floor so we can sit the hell down?"

"Language," Mabel chided, but elbowed Josh to move over. Several seconds of shuffling, muttering, and stifled giggles ensued, and then they were all squeezed in together, their little group of high-school misfits.

Well, almost all of them.

But then the fifth point in their star had faded so long ago, she barely felt its absence—until now. Sam was a void. A vanished link in their chain that they'd all learned to work around, refusing to let its absence compromise their collective strength.

Sure, Saul had grown distant as his Wall Street career took off, and Josh had also left town for several years, but she'd always felt their energy hanging out there in the universe, available to her if she needed it. When Saul's father died, or when Josh got married, or when Ellie's mom was diagnosed with cancer, they'd come together to support each other without judgment or bitterness or hesitation. If the worst happened, she knew she could count on each of them to be there for her.

Like when she came home to the note from her soon-to-be ex-husband, and then Ellie pretended to faint at a work event so she could race over to Mabel's apartment with chocolate and wine. Or when Josh used his law-school connections to find her a top-notch, wildly expensive divorce lawyer who did the whole thing for free. Or when she couldn't get out of the lease on the luxury apartment her ex had insisted they move into, and Saul called the building manager from New York City and threatened to acquire the whole property company in a hostile takeover if they didn't let her leave.

She smiled at the memory of that last one, watching the color drain from the manager's face, a little intimidated herself by Saul's scary, private-equity-hotshot demeanor. Then she'd taken the phone off speaker and heard him laughing so hard that she started, too, and didn't stop until she was halfway down the hall, signed copy of her terminated lease in hand.

She had good friends, she reflected with a contented sigh. Hopefully that would see her through this next phase of her life, as she finally stopped searching and waited for love to find her instead.

Josh's elbow dug into her ribs, popping her pleasant bubble.

"Over there. Look who it is," he hissed, jutting his chin toward the right-hand side.

Mabel followed the line of Josh's gaze, and suddenly her throat was packed with rocks, sharp and thick and threatening a landslide.

Sam stood uncertainly at the back of the aisle, scanning the pews for an empty seat.

The last time she'd seen him felt so final, she'd spent every hour since relegating him to the past from which he'd so unexpectedly and briefly reappeared. She'd focused on closure, on being grateful they'd had a chance to set things right, and on optimism for the future. It had to be a sign, right? The last rope tying her to her old ways suddenly coiling around her, bearing a sharp, gleaming knife, an invitation to sever that bond forever.

She'd made peace with Sam. She'd also had all the assurance she needed that he hadn't changed, and could never offer her the future she wanted. Goodbye should've been easy this time. Short and sweet.

So why did the mere sight of him make her all those rocks in her throat roll down to flatten her lungs?

Sam took a step forward, and then paused, most likely debating whether or not to ask Mrs. Morton to move her purse so he could sit down.

"Move over," she whispered to Josh.

"For him? No way."

"Don't be an ass." She shifted in the opposite direction

to make space, the butt-scooching equivalent of dominos as then Ellie's interest was piqued, followed in short order by Saul's.

"He's got some nerve," Ellie muttered at Mabel's side. Saul simply scowled before returning his attention to the rabbi, his expression imperiously disinterested.

"I told you, we talked things through," Mabel insisted, but Ellie arched a skeptical brow and didn't move an inch.

Exasperated, Mabel turned back to Josh. "Come on, there's plenty of room."

Josh crossed his arms and stared straight ahead. Mabel leaned around him to cast a pleading glance at his wife, Hanh, who shrugged.

After another moment's hesitation Sam leaned down—way down, had he always been so deliciously tall?—and spoke to Mrs. Morton. Mabel could see the astonished flash of recognition on her face before she plucked up her purse and set it on her lap, leaving just enough space for Sam to squeeze in beside her.

Once he was seated Mabel could only see his back, his broad shoulders putting the stretch in that chambray shirt to the test. Mrs. Morton kept stealing glances at him, and she knew it was only a matter of time before she whispered something to her husband, who'd nudge the woman beside him, and soon all of the decades-long veterans of Temple Sinai would be doing their level best to discreetly confirm the presence of Sam Strauss.

Meanwhile he kept his attention on the rabbi, his spine rigid, his posture confident.

The rocks in her chest transformed into embers, warm and glowing, a wisp of smoke singeing her windpipe and bringing tears to her eyes.

She was so proud of him.

He didn't have to be here. He could've stayed at home, quietly welcoming the New Year with a loaf of challah, a glass of red wine, and a pair of candles.

Instead he'd waded out into a community where, if not necessarily the *persona non grata* he thought he was, he certainly remained a figure of interest. Already heads were turning in his direction with various degrees of subtlety, and she knew as well as he did there'd be no escaping the hundred nosy questions he'd be peppered with as soon as the service concluded.

She wasn't sure exactly why he'd opted to come. She didn't know why he was still in Orchard Hill at all, since he could've easily left as soon as he appointed the realtor. She suspected it had something to do with honor, and owning mistakes, and making amends, and for that, she respected the hell out of him.

Mabel managed to take in only a fraction of the rest of the service, so lost in her personal mind-spiral that she barely caught one word in five, but she did find the wherewithal to tune in to the very end.

"And as we open the month of Tishrei, and indeed the

New Year, I'd like to ask each of you to recall your happiest moment in the year now ending. When were you so buoyant with joy that your feet barely touched the ground? Upon the birth of a grandchild, maybe? As you walked across a graduation stage? Or was it somewhere simpler—watching a mother duck guide her ducklings into a pond, or catching a glimpse of a golden sunrise on your way to work."

Mabel inhaled, flipping through a rapid-fire mental slideshow of the last twelve months. Moments of happiness like Rabbi Spellman described had been few and far between, if she was honest with herself, but she found a couple.

At Josh's house, flushed from a little red-wine buzz, laughing with her friends during the second night of Passover.

Cutting the ribbon on the expanded birth center, and then giving a dewy-eyed thank-you speech to the group of administrators, patients, and doctors who'd helped her get the midwifery program off the ground.

Kissing Sam.

Whoa, hold up there, girl. But her mental scolding couldn't suppress the memory of his lips against hers, his soft hair between her fingers, those few moments of weightless contentment in which the future and the past were as inconsequential as a breath of air stirring a leaf.

"Now I want you to take all of that happiness, every inch of your smile, every second of your elation, and silently give it away to the person you think needs it most," the rabbi instructed.

Mabel closed her eyes and imagined rolling those instances of joy into a ball, silver and shining. Her default reaction was to toss it to her mom, who for all her successes in life remained downbeat and lonely in her singleness, even if she would never admit it.

But then she thought of the shadows in Sam's eyes. His reluctance to admit that he was in pain. The hollowness in his voice when he talked about his career. The disconnect between his casual insistence that everything in his life was going to plan and his faraway expression when he thought she wasn't looking.

Here you go. Hope it helps. In her mind's eye she cupped the ball in two hands and passed it to him, his much bigger palm closing over it.

Then she opened her eyes and discovered Sam had twisted around to look at her.

He smiled. She smiled, too.

He turned back to face the front and she knew, without a shadow of a doubt, that they'd just traded bliss.

An ember glowed inside her again, but this one was in the pit of her stomach, and instead of fading from a fire long extinguished, it was just beginning to spark into life.

The service ended, and exactly as Mabel predicted, Sam was barely out of his seat when the first set of old-school Temple Sinai devotees approached him. By the time she'd shuffled out of her own packed pew he was surrounded by people from their parents' cohort and older, including the legendarily flirty ninety-four-year-old Mrs. Finkelstein, whose friendly pats on his back were veering dangerously low on his waist.

"And now we have my favorite part of every Temple Sinai occasion—the nosh." Hanh rubbed her hands together gleefully. She motioned to Eve, Saul's girlfriend, and the two of them joined the slow-moving stream of people heading out of the sanctuary.

"I'll meet you guys in the social hall. I need to go rescue Sam," she told Josh, who stopped her with a hand on her forearm.

"Do you?" he asked, brows raised above his glasses.

"He can take care of himself," Saul added coldly, glancing past her at the cluster around Sam. Ellie stood beside him, her crossed arms echoing his displeasure.

Mabel propped her hands on her hips. "Was I the only one listening to Rabbi Spellman? It's Rosh Ha-freaking-shanah, guys. Time for renewal and forgiveness and doing better, not clinging to grudges from high school. Not to mention, if anyone has a right to be mad, it's me. If I'm cool with him, the rest of you should be, too."

The three of them exchanged uncertain glances while Mabel continued to glare at them, making her annoyance plain.

Finally Josh heaved a reluctant sigh. "Maybe we can give him a chance."

"But it's his last one, and he better not screw it up," Saul said sharply.

Ellie pressed her mouth into a worried line. "We just don't want you to get hurt again."

"I won't," Mabel declared confidently. "Anyway, he's leaving soon, and I'm retiring from the dating game. We're friends. That's it."

Skepticism shined its icy brilliance on all three of her dearest, most loyal friends' faces so intensely that it chilled her, a cold shiver shimmying down her torso and crystallizing at the base of her spine.

Without another word she turned on her heel, leaving them to cluck their tongues or shake their heads or whatever busybody nonsense would make them feel better. She was choosing forgiveness and positivity, and if they couldn't get on board, that wasn't her problem.

She reached Sam in a few quick strides. His back was turned, so she snaked her arm around his elbow and tugged him toward her.

"Hey, fancy meeting..." The words died in her throat as he pivoted enough for her to see which of Temple Sinai's finest had been occupying him when she arrived.

Her mom.

"Hi, sweetie. I'd better go help with the food. See you both later." Her mother's smile was sheepish as she edged past them, hurrying to catch up with the rest of the congregation.

Sam watched her mom leave, and Mabel poked him in the ribs to get his attention. "What was that about?"

"You'll never believe me."

"Tell me."

Sam lowered his gaze to meet hers, his lips quirked up in a bemused smile. "She asked for my dad's number."

"You're kidding." Mabel whipped her head back toward where her mom had just been, but she was long gone.

Guess that conversation would have to wait—but not for long, if Mabel had her way.

"Maybe she wants to deliver her happiness verbally," Sam suggested drily.

"Maybe we've inspired her to make amends," Mabel countered, only half joking.

That was the most likely explanation. After seeing the two of them salvage a friendship from their car-crash breakup, and with the safety of knowing a phone call wouldn't exacerbate Evelyn's constant suspicions, she probably wanted to finally have the discussion that would put her messy past with Leo behind her.

Good for her, Mabel decided. This was the season of starting over, after all.

"My goodness, Sam, what a pleasure it is to see you again. And Mabel. How are you, dear?" Mrs. Futter's gushing tone thinned to a trickle as she eyed Mabel's arm, still linked through Sam's.

"I'm fantastic, thank you for asking. How's…" Mabel

fumbled for the name of her son. "Richie?"

"Married," Mrs. Futter said primly. "How long will you be in town, Sam?"

"Another week or so. I just put my grandparents' house on the market."

"What a shame—Lauren is coming out for a visit next month. You're sure you won't be staying longer?"

"Afraid not."

"Oh well, maybe next time." Mrs. Futter patted his arm approvingly and made for the door.

"*Married*," Mabel mimicked in a nasal, officious voice. "Don't worry, Mrs. Futter, I'm not planning to seduce your son."

"Meanwhile she's trying to set me up with Lauren. I thought she had a baby with someone?"

"She did, and they're still happily together as far as I know, but they never got married, which must drive her mother up the wall. Also, he's French."

"No wonder I look like a decent alternative."

Mabel rolled her eyes. "Didn't I tell you that everyone would be happy to see you? Now look, you turn up to one service and women are throwing their daughters at you."

"You were right. You're always right. There, did that help?"

"Not really, but food will. Let's go before all the good stuff is gone."

Normally the social hall felt cavernous even during weekly Oneg Shabbat, but tonight it brimmed with activity. Congregants milled around the long tables laid with food, children dashed around the perimeter, and a series of people came in and out of the attached kitchen, refilling empty chafing dishes and adding to the already impressive spread. The room rang with the merry din of talking and laughter, and the hand-drawn decorations of cardboard shofars and crayon-colored apples rounded out the cozy, festive atmosphere.

Mabel spotted their high-school crew against the far wall, safely out of the way of the buffet traffic as they hoisted their paper plates to make room for the heads of Ellie's two nephews as they careened past.

Without thinking Mabel took Sam's hand to lead him through the crowded room, realizing only after several heads turned in their direction how that must look. Sam had to have noticed as well, but his grip stayed firm, his fingers loosening only when they reached their friends.

"How's the nosh?" Mabel asked brightly, ignoring everyone's pointed looks as she dropped Sam's hand.

Her question was met with stony silence. Hanh and Eve had the decency to look mildly embarrassed; Saul, Josh, and Ellie simply glared at Sam.

Sam leaned against the wall, propping his hip on the windowsill. Belatedly Mabel realized he'd been standing for at least fifteen minutes since the service ended, but if he was in pain, he kept it under wraps. He met his old friends' gazes levelly and openly, ready for whatever they had to say.

Eve glanced at Saul, disapproval slashed across her face, and then she bounded forward, hand extended.

"We haven't met—I'm Eve Klein, Saul's better half."

"Sam Strauss. It's a pleasure," he greeted her warmly, clasping her hand.

"And I'm Hanh. Josh talked me into marrying him a couple of years back." She smiled and gave a little wave.

"Nice to meet you, Hanh."

"What are you doing here, Sam?" Josh asked coldly.

Sam drew a deep, thoughtful breath. "Ostensibly I came back to town to sell my grandparents' house. I hadn't planned to do much else, just get the place tidy and go. But then I ran into Mabel—"

"You mean you opted into a media blitz alongside her, capitalizing on your former relationship to keep yourself in the spotlight," Saul interjected.

"You know damn well the publicity stuff was all my idea, to add some height to my midwifery soapbox," she countered. "I had to talk him into it."

Saul narrowed his eyes.

"I guess I realized that I could use this time to do more than close out my family's history in Orchard Hill—I could repair some of my own history, too. Mabel and I have talked a lot about what happened that summer, and I think we're okay. Aren't we?"

"We're okay," she confirmed, and he flashed her a thousand-watt smile that lit her up inside like summer lightning.

"At the same time, I know I owe each of you an apology, too. Not just for hurting someone you care about, but for dropping off the map and generally being a crappy friend."

"You weren't a crappy friend, Sam, you were nonexistent. That's much worse," Josh told him.

"I know," Sam agreed sincerely. "I was young and stupid, and I told myself it'd be better to start college with a blank slate. The truth is I wasn't mature enough then to own the way I broke up with Mabel, but I am now. I won't ask any of you to forgive me, but I will say I screwed up, and I'm sorry."

An uneasy silence followed. Mabel could see her friends shifting their weight, avoiding Sam's eyes, and fidgeting with their plastic forks as they processed his apology and decided what to do next.

Funny to think she was the one standing beside him, championing him to her critical friends, when she had more reason than any of them to hold a grudge. She really had forgiven him, though, and she stood a little taller, proud of herself for refusing to waste any more energy on that old, scarred-over wound.

Josh shuffled his feet, but her money was on Ellie breaking first. The last couple of years had hardened her a bit, but inside she still had the softest heart Mabel had ever known. She wouldn't stay mad at Sam.

Josh would fold pretty quickly afterward—he hated confrontation. Saul would take the longest, and it might not happen today at all, but she was sure he'd get there, too.

They might not ever recover who they all were twelve years ago, but it'd be an awful lot more than they had yesterday.

"Apology accepted," Saul announced suddenly. He stuck his paper plate on the windowsill, took two steps forward, and pulled Sam into a quick, tight hug.

"We've all screwed up, one way or another," she heard Saul murmur to his old friend before he let go.

Josh rolled his eyes. "Oh, fine, I guess we'll let you back into the fold. And by fold I mean WhatsApp group used almost exclusively to circulate funny memes. *Really* funny ones, Strauss. We have a high bar."

Mabel smiled at the relief audible in Josh's voice. He was probably grateful that Saul made the first move so he didn't have to, and for the cessation of tensions. He might be tough in the courtroom, but off-duty Josh despised conflict and aggression.

Ellie surprised her, though. She'd actually taken a step back, watching Saul and Josh warily. Her gaze snagged on Mabel's, and then she looked away hurriedly, craning her neck as she scanned the room.

"I think Jonah needs me. I'll see you all later, okay?"

Mabel followed Ellie's line of sight to find Jonah frowning at two slightly different dishes of green beans—one with pomegranate seeds, one with honey mustard sauce.

"He's got a big decision to make but I'm sure he'll…" Mabel trailed off as Ellie walked away, her stride short and urgent.

"Anyway, Sam, tell us what you've done with your life," Josh said quickly, before the awkwardness of Ellie's departure had a chance to take root.

Mabel watched Ellie take Jonah's arm and push up on her toes to say something in his ear. He nodded, and the two of them left the social hall.

For a few moments Mabel stared at the space Ellie had just vacated, trying to figure out what happened. Then Josh laughed at something Sam said, and Eve added an even funnier, more sarcastic response, and Mabel put Ellie's discomfort to one side. She'd try to catch her later and talk through whatever was bothering her, but for now, she wanted to enjoy this rare time with her friends.

The ease with which Sam slotted back into their rhythm would've astonished her if she hadn't already experienced it firsthand. Sometimes it was hard to believe that twelve years had passed since they'd all been together like this, or that so much of that intervening decade had been wasted on bitterness and resentment.

If anything, she regretted not convening everyone sooner. Maybe she could throw a dinner party before Sam left, to strengthen these fresh bonds before they were once again tested by absence. Maybe she could even convince him to spend an extra week or two in town. Her heart trembled with girlish giddiness as she considered the possibilities. Sukkot was coming, followed by all the secular events and festivals that marked autumn's arrival. They could have a fall picnic with apple cider and pumpkin pie, or help Josh build a sukkah in his yard, and then have dinner under—

"Where to next?" Hanh asked Sam, tugging Mabel out of her festive seasonal fantasies.

"Helsinki. I just got the assignment today."

Mabel could swear there was apology in Sam's eyes as they swept across her face, but then she was finding it hard to focus on anything except the jagged disappointment working its way down her throat.

"Since when is Finland a war zone?" Saul asked.

"It's not. I'll be working with the local authorities on a refugee resettlement program. It's sort of a respite posting, after… To make sure I don't get burned out," he replied, and Mabel realized he hadn't mentioned the car accident at all.

"It's a standard rotation," he added, ignoring her curious gaze. "The upside is I can actually host visitors for once. No Kevlar required."

Hanh's eyes lit up. "Don't they do heli-skiing in Finland?"

"No. Absolutely not." Josh shook his head.

The discussion devolved into good-natured banter about extreme sports, and Mabel doubted anyone paid much attention when Sam muttered something about getting a drink, weaved through the crowd, and slipped out of the hall.

Her immediate instinct was to chase after him, and so she forced herself to stay put. This was Erev Rosh Hashanah, and her resolution was in full effect. No more running after men who couldn't—or wouldn't—ask for what she had to offer.

But as the minutes ticked by she started to pick through her own terms and conditions. Did this new policy apply only to romantic interests, or all men everywhere? If her dad suddenly reappeared after years of silence, and opened the door to communication but didn't explicitly invite her to engage, would she make the first move? Reconnecting with Sam had driven home the pointlessness of wasting time and energy on bad blood—would her no-chasing policy lead her to make the same mistake if she didn't leave room for context and nuance?

The resolution is officially amended to apply only to would-be suitors, she declared to herself. As her friend, and only her friend, Sam was thereby exempt.

She pushed off the wall and headed for the door.

She was halfway across the room when someone grabbed her arm.

"Ellie," Mabel greeted her friend, whose brow was pinched. "You disappeared."

"Don't run after him. Let him go."

"I don't know what you're talking about." Mabel tugged

her arm free, because of course she knew exactly who Ellie meant.

"He left you once, and he'll do it again. Don't break your promise to yourself."

"I'm not doing anything wrong," Mabel shot back, and for a split second she was in the apartment above the flower shop, trying not to wither under her mother's accusatory gaze, insisting it was a coincidence that she and Sam came out of the library at the same time, knowing full well she'd be wearing collared shirts for days to hide the dark-red hickey on her neck.

Except Ellie really did want the best for her, and the hurt in her expression made Mabel regret her defensive tone.

"Sorry, Els, but I'm beyond done with people telling me what to do when it comes to Sam. I know he's leaving, and I'm—"

Not falling for him.

Why couldn't she say it? It was true—wasn't it?

"I'm fine. Okay?"

"Okay," Ellie said softly.

Mabel turned her back on her friend's lingering, skeptical gaze, snagged a plate of the honey-drizzled apple slices that had just been set out, then made her way through the belly of Temple Sinai to the place she knew she'd find Sam.

Temple Sinai was a single-story building, but the double-height ceilings in the sanctuary and the social hall created a void space over the offices and classrooms. The long, nearly windowless room was only accessible via a pull-down ladder in the storage room, and at its far end a single frosted-glass window opened onto another ladder, which led straight up to the roof.

She and Sam had discovered this hidden pathway by accident one wintry December evening, when they'd each slipped out of the annual Hanukkah-play performance and stolen into the storage room to make out. That night the risk of discovery was heightened with most of the congregation packed into the sanctuary, and as a result so was their lust for each other.

Mabel smiled as she crossed the now brightly lit storage room, remembering their hot, frantic fumbling in the pitch dark, the way they'd frozen in place after she'd accidentally kicked a plastic bucket across the room, terrified the racket would summon a curious adult. But the play's sweet, off-key singing gave them the cover they needed, and when Sam inadvertently put his elbow through the ladder someone had left descended, they saw no reason not to follow where it led.

She switched off the light as she put her foot on the first rung, and as she climbed out of the near-complete darkness she could almost hear them, two teenagers high on love and rebellion, stifling giggles, smiling through the deep shadows.

She was older now, and the second, narrower ladder to the roof wasn't quite as easy to climb as she remembered, especially with a paper plate jammed between her teeth. But she made it to the roof, and wasn't the least bit surprised to find Sam exactly where she'd seen him so many times—perched on a disconnected air-conditioning unit, staring up at the stars.

"Thought I might find you here." Mabel sat beside him, setting down the paper plate.

"I needed a break. Aren't you cold?"

Now that he mentioned it, there was definitely a bite in the September evening air. She'd left her jacket in the overheated social hall, and she shivered as goose bumps rippled beneath the thin sleeves of her top.

Without a word Sam put his arm across her shoulders and scooped her against his side. She snuggled in tightly, letting the heat from his big body warm her chilled flesh.

"I'm glad you put things right with Saul and Josh."

"Ellie's still mad."

"I'll work on her," Mabel promised.

He shook his head. "There's only one thing I need you to do."

"Which is?"

"Forgive me."

Her head snapped up. Sam was watching her intently, the tension in his jaw echoed in the arm still clutching her to his side. His eyes were wide, at once hopeful and pleading, and in the rapidly fading dusk she could see the reflection of Orchard Hill's humble skyline. Little dots of light scattered across his irises, a map of their shared history.

Their story couldn't be rewritten. But it wasn't over, either.

She put her palm on his cheek. Let her thumb smooth the hair at his temple.

"I forgive you, Sam. Of course I do."

He exhaled so completely she would've believed he'd been holding that breath for twelve years. Then he buried his face in the crook of her neck and she wrapped her arms around his head, plunging her fingers into his hair.

"I'm sorry, Mabel," he whispered, the words hot against her skin.

"It's okay," she told him, and it was. For the first time in her adult life, it really was.

She prodded the edges of the wound she'd carried for a decade, testing for tender spots, for areas that were still raw, for any indication that she wasn't finally healed and whole.

She found nothing but seamless perfection.

Sam's fingers tangled in her hair, his stubble rasping against her neck. Her name was a fevered murmur beside her ear and then his mouth was on hers.

She drank in his kiss, the years of doubt and pain and crushing rejection and outright marital failure slipping off her shoulders like a heavy, oversized coat puddling on the floor at her feet. The night was cold but those embers in her chest glowed to life, that spark of pride when she'd first seen Sam in the temple flickering into golden flames, steady and strong.

All that energy spent on keeping them apart, the threats,

the screaming, the relentless visitation of old hurts on a generation that hadn't earned them, and here they were. Two hearts caught in an inescapable gravitational pull, incapable of keeping apart, impossible to knit together.

Her breath hitched in her throat and she kissed Sam harder, desperate to sink into this moment and ignore its limits, to pretend this could be their forever, to fool herself that this was anything other than another goodbye.

Too late. Sam either sensed the root of her need or shared it, because he swept his tongue along her lower lip once more, softly, sweetly, and then gently parted their mouths.

He pressed his forehead to hers, cognac-colored lashes fanning against his cheeks as he closed his eyes.

"What are we doing, Mabel?"

"Whatever we want," she replied, but it came out breathy and insubstantial.

He took her face in his hands, fixing her with that stormy-sea gaze.

"Can I tell you why I really came back to town?"

"You can tell me anything."

"After the accident, I had no one to call. No friends, no girlfriend, not even a colleague I knew well enough to ask for help."

You could've called me, she wanted to say, but of course he couldn't. Not then.

"For years I'd been alone. I moved around, I stayed busy,

and that was enough—I didn't need anyone. But in the back of that ambulance, for the first time, I felt it. I wasn't just alone—I was lonely."

She nodded slowly, imagining him by himself, in pain, unable even to reach out to the parents who'd never been soft, never been understanding, who'd offered little more than brittle pats on the back whenever he'd been sick or injured.

"So you came back to Orchard Hill to reconnect with the people here?" she asked.

He shook his head, dropping his hands. "Not initially. I came back to connect with myself. Somewhere along the way I lost him—that ambitious, idealistic kid with good friends and big dreams. I thought if I could be here for a little while, leaf through that history, dwell in this place that made me, maybe he'd resurface. Maybe I could remember how to crack the door just enough to let people in."

"Has it worked?"

"Yes and no." He smiled. "I don't think I needed to connect with my old self at all. I needed to connect with you."

Her heart bobbed in her throat. "Really?"

He nodded. "Breaking up with you was the first betrayal—the first time I turned away from who I'm meant to be. I never should've hurt you like that, Mabel. I didn't realize it until now, but I needed to come back and fix it."

"You fixed it," she assured him, although even as the words left her mouth she suspected they might be the ones that severed this tenuous link they'd formed and sent them drifting in opposite directions once more.

"I hope so. Because I can't stay much longer."

There it was. He was leaving her.

Again.

She had no right to be annoyed, had never been under any impression he was here to stay. Nonetheless she let a wave of indignation and anger buoy her up and then plunge her back to earth, gripping the cold, sharp edge of the air conditioner in a feeble effort to keep herself upright.

"Well," she said flatly, reaching around to grab the plate of apples and honey. She shifted aside, making room to set it between them—and positioning herself safely out of range of his scent, his heat, and the vital energy that had always radiated from him like steam off a winter-morning swimmer.

"Here's to a New Year," she said, raising an apple slice. "May we both find what we're looking for."

"May what you're looking for find you," he corrected, taking a slice and knocking it against hers. "Happy New Year, Mabel."

"Happy New Year, Sam."

The apple was sweet, the honey sweeter, and the flesh made extra cold by the nighttime air crunched delightfully between her teeth.

She finished the first slice and took a second. It was even more delicious than the first.

But not nearly sweet enough to drive the bitter taste from her mouth.

Chapter Nine

Babies are in no hurry to be born today! On my way now, be there in ten.

Sam closed the text from Mabel, popped in his earbuds, and flicked to the TV show he'd downloaded earlier that day. The unseasonal cold front meant he was the only person in the courtyard café at Second Chance, a boutique gift store on Main Street, but that suited him just fine. He only had a few days left in his hometown, and he was finally allowing himself to enjoy it.

He hadn't seen Mabel since Erev Rosh Hashanah, but he'd relived their conversation—and their kiss—almost constantly.

He was in dangerous territory. On one hand, he was perfectly poised to walk away, once and for all. He had her forgiveness, her friendship, the closure he needed. He should draw a line under this experience and move forward toward the life he wanted.

On the other hand…he didn't want to.

The longer he spent with Mabel, the more addicted to her he became. That wasn't fair to her, and it wasn't right for him. He needed to use this period of recovery and rediscovery to be better, to open himself up, to knock a few cracks in his walls and accept that with the drafts came light. He wasn't sure when—or if—he'd ever be ready to walk down the aisle, but he was done being alone.

Meanwhile Mabel deserved devotion, the sort of man who would treasure her and fight for her—the opposite of who he'd been when they broke up, and the ideal from which he was still a long way off. She wanted to jump into commitment with both feet, when he'd only just decided to kneel by the edge and test the water. What if he couldn't handle it? What if he screwed it up? As much as he hated to admit it, he hadn't forgotten his father's warning. He'd already hurt her once—he didn't trust himself not to do it again.

And yet none of those reasons managed to overwhelm his attraction. Sometimes his thoughts wandered as far as proposing a no-strings fling, just a couple of nights to satisfy their cravings—and then he reminded himself he'd already done enough damage for a lifetime, and the last thing she needed was another man loving and leaving her.

Not that he loved her, of course.

Although if he wasn't careful, he might.

Despite being tempted several times in the last few days, he'd managed not to text or call Mabel. But when she asked him to meet her at Second Chance with just a few hours' notice, he agreed right away.

"Dangerous territory," he reiterated to himself, taking a sip of coffee before tapping play on the video. Any misstep and he'd lose Mabel forever. She'd forgiven him once—she wouldn't do it again.

He zipped his coat up to his chin and focused on the screen. The evening dusk and the unusually frigid temperature added to the TV show's atmosphere, so by the time Mabel tapped him on the shoulder he was so engrossed in the story he startled.

"What are you watching?" she asked, leaning over his shoulder to frown at the concave-cheeked man scowling on the screen.

"A Nordic mystery. I think it might be Danish."

"Any good?"

"Sort of. It's research."

"On how to hide a body in the fjords?"

"And get away with it, more crucially. Did you order already?" He stuffed his earbuds in his pocket as Mabel settled into the seat on the other side of the snug, wrought-iron café table.

"I did, on my way in."

"This is a cool place," he remarked. Twinkle lights draped over the trellis above them, and glass-and-iron lanterns glowed at intervals along the courtyard's perimeter. The darker the sky above them, the more secretive and special this place felt, like a hidden garden that only they knew about.

"Isn't it? Can you believe this used to be that musty old thrift store? The owner, Noa, is such a gem. It's pretty empty in there—I hope the business is doing okay. She only opened this café section in the spring, so it hasn't survived a winter yet, and if tonight is any indication, we're in for a frosty one."

"We're doing our part to keep it going, in any case. What did you want to talk to me about?"

"Straight to the point as usual."

The back door creaked open and Noa appeared with a steaming teapot, a teacup, and a saucer all made from the same delicately patterned china. Mabel accepted her drink gratefully, made a little small talk about the weather, and then waited until Noa was safely back inside before turning to Sam with intent in her eyes.

"I need to ask you for a favor."

"Go for it."

"A big favor."

"What is it?" he asked cautiously.

"I've gotten another interview request. A big one."

"How big?"

"Flying-us-to-New-York big."

"I can't. I've already booked my flight back to DC." He exhaled, relieved to have such an immutable, easy excuse within reach.

"Not until next week, though, right? Because they want us there the day after tomorrow."

"Come on, Mabel," he responded, unable to keep the exasperation from his voice. "How would that even be possible? What do they want us to do, jump on a plane at twenty-four hours' notice?"

"Actually, yes."

He opened his mouth to object, but she held up a hand to silence him.

"I know it's a lot to ask, but I will never get an opportunity like this again. This isn't just a quick segment—we'll be the primary guests on one of the biggest network shows in the country. Please tell me you've heard of *Your New Life* with Paige Harris."

"Of course I haven't," he replied irritably.

"She's got a PhD in something, psychology maybe, and every week she counsels someone who needs help or interviews interesting people. It's kind of a self-help, uplifting vibe. It's really good—you should watch it," she told him pointedly.

"Think I'll stick with the Danish detective show."

She rolled her eyes. "Anyway, the producers love our story, especially because we both have service-oriented careers. They want us to talk about the compulsion to serve, what motivates us, how we push through the hard times—not just the relationship angle."

He was shaking his head before she finished speaking. "I'm sorry, Mabel, I can't go on TV and be the poster boy for international aid. I'm only just getting back on my feet, being confident in who I am and what I'm doing. And my boss must feel it, too, or he wouldn't be sending me to hold bureaucratic hands in Helsinki."

It took a few seconds of Mabel's shocked silence for him to realize what he'd just said—and to whom. That first night in his grandmother's living room he'd been so careful to manage her perception of him, controlling what he shared with the same ruthless efficiency he applied to natural disasters and conflict zones, so used to self-censoring that it came instinctively.

Yet in just a couple of weeks she'd crept through his defenses, quietly pried him open until he was blurting out deeply buried truths and airing his pain without a second thought.

Here he thought he had all this work to do to put a couple of chinks in his walls, meanwhile Mabel smashed straight through and he hadn't even noticed.

Saying out loud what he'd been struggling to articulate to himself hurt more than he expected, but Mabel's understanding nod helped. Helped a lot.

"There's no shame in easing back into work after a much-needed break. Your boss probably just wants to set you up for success, make sure he's not throwing you in at the deep end."

He shrugged, still reeling from his disclosure, not wanting to go any further down this line of conversation.

Mabel watched him thoughtfully for another few seconds, then sighed.

"Here's the situation. The administrators at my hospital are weeks away from deciding whether to fund an expansion for the midwifery program. If I get it right, this level of media attention might just be the final push they need. I can take the lead—I can talk ninety-nine percent of the time, if that'll get you to agree. I have to do this, Sam. My life is not high-flying and global like yours. This is a once-in-a-career chance for me, and I cannot let it pass me by."

She stared at him so intensely, so pleadingly, he almost smiled. She had no idea the effect she had on him—or that she was the only person in the world who threatened his ability to say no.

The trip would be long and hard and uncomfortable, but he'd do it for her. He'd do anything for her.

Almost.

"You win. I'll do it."

She clapped her hands together. "Really?"

He nodded, and she leapt out of her seat to practically fall into his lap, throwing her arms around his neck.

"You have no idea how much this means to me, Sam. Thank you. Thank you so much."

He held her tightly, too lost in her softness and her vanilla-and-tangerine scent to find words—at least not any words he could bring himself to say, no matter how honest they might be.

Like: *Your happiness feels so much more important than my*

own. Or: *You're the only person I've ever imagined a future with.* And above all: *I'm sorry I can never give you everything you deserve.*

Holding Mabel was like clutching a grenade with its pin halfway out. Nothing and no one had ever tempted him like she did, tugging him down a path he knew would end in agony for them both.

Although he still struggled to visualize it, he resolved to try dating once he got to Helsinki. Maybe he could find a woman who was different to Mabel, someone less devoted, who didn't throw herself wholeheartedly into everything she did, and who wanted a relationship with some healthy distance instead of the all-consuming, pulse-quickening love he and Mabel had shared.

Because he had loved her, and he'd never truly stopped, just learned to wrap it in guilt and ambition and stalwart refusal until he couldn't see the beating heart beneath.

This trip home had shredded enough of what kept his enduring love for Mabel concealed. He needed to snuff it out once and for all, or his father's long-ago prophecy would finally—and painfully—come to fruition.

Sam took her by the shoulders and held her at arm's length. His body keened at the loss, need for her burned in his stomach, but his grip was steady and strong.

"Send me the flight details," he told her firmly. "I'll go home and pack."

"Knock, knock." Mabel peered around the door, but the kitchen in her mother's apartment was dark. The whole place looked unusually uninhabited, and she stepped all the way inside, closing the door behind her.

Her mom hadn't told her she had plans tonight—not that she had to, Mabel supposed. Growing up without a man in the house meant they'd always been closer than your average mom-and-daughter pair, but Mabel had been keeping her distance since Sam reappeared, and in retrospect she realized her mom had withdrawn a little, too.

It made sense—neither of them were in a hurry to reopen that old wound. And as much as Mabel wanted to finally get it all out in the open before she went on an overnight trip with Sam, part of her secretly hoped her mom wasn't home, and they could delay this conversation until she got back from New York.

New York City. Just the idea of it thrilled her as she moved through the apartment, checking for any signs of life. Excluding a messy girls' trip to South Padre Island and the long weekend she and her mom spent in Tampa, she'd barely left the state, and had never been anywhere as big or glamorous as New York. And to have Sam at her side to explore all those busy streets and bright lights… But these were the final few days of this brief reconnection, and it'd serve her well to remember that.

"Mom?" she called as she crossed the empty sitting room. A second later she heard a muffled crash from her mom's bedroom and headed in that direction.

She found her mom stepping out of her walk-in closet, and spotted a step stool inside in the instant before her mom shut the door.

"Everything okay?"

"Fine." Norma smiled brightly. "I didn't know you'd be stopping by tonight. What's up?"

"Unexpected development in my moment of viral fame. Can we sit down?"

"Sure." Her mom perched on the end of her bed and patted the space beside her.

"You know that show *Your New Life*?"

"Of course."

"They called today. They want Sam and me to appear as guests. They'll fly us to New York and everything."

Norma's eyes widened. "Wow. When?"

"Tomorrow."

"Tomorrow?" her mom echoed in a high, squeezed voice.

Mabel nodded.

Norma's expression became determined. "This is a huge opportunity—we have to do whatever we can to get you on that plane. What do you need? Can you get time off work? Should I drive you to the airport?"

"It's all good, Mom," Mabel assured her with a fond smile. Norma may not have been able to give her the life she wanted, but she'd never, ever stood in the way of her dreams.

Well, except for one.

"The logistics are all set," she continued. "But I wanted to talk to you about Sam."

Norma sighed, adjusting her posture to signal she was settling in for the long haul. "I guess we're overdue for this discussion."

"We are, and it's one we should have before he and I spend three days traveling together."

"Okay." Norma sat up straight. "Shoot."

In for a penny… "I know you apologized to him."

Mabel thought that revelation would at least rattle her mom, but Norma simply nodded.

"That wasn't a secret?"

"I figured he'd tell you. His loyalty is to you, after all."

"I wouldn't go that far."

"Oh, I think it is."

Mabel shook her head dismissively, set on keeping this conversation on track. "Regardless, he told me what you said, and I'd like to know why you said it."

Her mom tilted her head sympathetically. "I know I owe you an apology, too. I was waiting for the right time, and I suppose this is as good as any."

Norma inhaled, sitting up straighter. "I'm sorry, Mabel. If it could do it all differently, relive those years you were a teenager, I would."

At first Mabel could do no more than stare at her mother

while an epic emotional battle raged within her rib cage. Resignation fought hysteria, forgiveness warred with resentment, and her grown-up awareness that nothing could change the past had a knife to its throat, wielded by an immature, bitter, and ferocious refusal to let go of the suffering that had shaped so much of her adult life.

Unfortunately, the latter won.

"You should be sorry," Mabel told her mother hotly, instantly embarrassed by her petulant tone but totally unable to roll it back, her logical mind now merely an observer as a lava flow of pent-up hurt poured up and out of the core of her soul.

"What happened before Sam and I were born should've had nothing to do with us," Mabel said pointedly.

"I know, sweetie, and I—"

"No, you don't know. Sam and I started dating in seventh grade, and were together all through high school. Do you have any idea how hard it was to keep that quiet? How stressful? How much we both hated lying to our parents, but wanted each other more than we wanted to be honest?"

Her mom's expression was pinched. "I'm sorry you felt you had to sneak around."

"Sneak around," Mabel echoed with a hollow, incredulous laugh. "The three of you forced us to live a lie. We had entire schedules of made-up extracurriculars. Our friends had to cover for us, lying to you, lying to their own parents so no one would know we'd been in the same place at the same time. We went to both proms together and we don't even have a single photo of the two of us. I *loved* him, Mom, and instead of being happy I felt guilty and ashamed."

For the briefest of instants Mabel felt triumphant. Vindicated. As if she'd finally finished pushing a boulder up the steep rise of a hill and used the last wisp of her strength to shove it off the edge and watch it tumble into the deep valley below. She was shaky with spent adrenaline, breathless and tired, but for the first time in twelve years her shoulders rose and fell easily, freed from the burden they'd carried.

Then Norma's lower lip trembled, tears glimmered in her eyes, and Mabel thought she might be the meanest, most ungrateful daughter in the entire world.

"I'm sorry, Mom, I didn't—"

"Don't you dare apologize," Norma cut her off sharply, the characteristic steel back in her tone. "This was my fault. I always tried to strike a balance between being strict and also being open, so you'd come to me with your problems, but if you were this afraid to tell me about Sam, then I got it all wrong."

Mabel shook her head furiously at her mother's misapprehension of the situation.

"We didn't hide our relationship from you because we were scared of punishment," she explained. "We hid it because we didn't want to hurt you. Any of you."

Norma simply stared at her, mouth half-open in disbelief.

"Even when this viral publicity thing happened, Sam brought up the effect it might have on the three of you," she continued. "We knew it was an open wound for you all. We didn't want to make it worse."

"Mabel," her mother murmured. She pressed her fingers against her temples, something she often did at work when faced with a complicated problem, and Mabel wondered if her mother thought there might still be a solution, that after all these years and all this pain, she might still be able to heal her daughter's heart.

Sorrow seared Mabel's throat, leaving it rough and raw.

There'd be no fixing this. Whatever she thought she could do, it was way too late.

"I didn't realize the full extent of the damage we'd caused," her mom said finally, dropping her hand and looking Mabel squarely in the eyes. "Me, and Leo, and Evelyn. Now that I put it all together—the breakup, the boyfriends, the divorce—I see the true cost. I thought I was doing the right thing by trying to keep you two apart—that I was protecting you from the heartbreak I suffered with his father. Instead I drove you away from a man who loved you so much that he was willing to betray his parents' wishes to choose you. I'm not sure I'll ever forgive myself for that, and I won't ask you to forgive me, either."

"It's okay, Mom," Mabel told her softly—and suddenly, it was. Peace descended over her body, filling the hole from which she'd excavated that boulder of long-held anguish.

She'd shared her truth, her mom had listened, and that was enough.

She reached across the bed and took her mom's hand, squeezing it tightly. Norma smiled reluctantly.

"You know I love you more than anything, baby girl. I'm sorry I messed up. If there's anything I can do to help you fix things with Sam, just say the word."

"Thanks, Mom," Mabel said sincerely. "But Sam and I are over. Maybe he did love me once, but he's not the hero you think he is. He told me back then that he didn't want a relationship, and he feels the same way now. He wasn't the one who would've stayed—he was the first one to leave. I fell for him, and he left, and that's set the tone for every other relationship I've ever had. I always thought you were wrong to interfere, but in the long run, maybe it would've been better if I'd listened."

"Oh, honey." Her mom grabbed her hand, squeezing it tightly. "He wasn't the first one who left you. That was your dad."

Tears spilled down Mabel's cheeks, hot and unexpected, at the mention of a man who'd always loomed large in the shadows of her life, yearned for, unknowable, and eternally unattainable. She didn't want this to be about him, because he was long gone, and whatever was wrong between them would never be put right.

"But that doesn't… It's not… This was all Sam's fault. I've forgiven him, but he's not innocent."

"Maybe his parents said something to make him change his mind," Norma suggested, reaching over to brush the tears from Mabel's face. "I saw his face when he was on your doorstep the other week. That wasn't just a friendly house call."

"Even if they pushed him at the time, he's been single ever since. Whatever happened that night stuck."

Norma shrugged. "And perhaps it can be unstuck."

"I doubt it. He doesn't want to wind up in a marriage like his parents', and I don't blame him," Mabel said bitterly, sniffing hard as she swiped the tears off her face. "His mom is an awful human being. She treated you like you were some unapologetic, aggressive homewrecker when you did nothing wrong. There are still people at shul who turn their noses up at us. If I'd grown up in a house like Sam's, I'd probably run from anything resembling commitment, too."

Her mom was quiet for so long that Mabel's attention drifted up, fixing on her mother with curiosity.

"Mabel," Norma began, and then stopped, studying her hands in her lap. She took a breath, released it, and repeated the same again twice before finally raising her gaze to meet her daughter's.

"Leo and I had an affair."

Mabel blinked repeatedly, unsuccessfully trying to wake herself up from what had to be a spectacularly vivid dream.

"You what?" she managed eventually.

"I'm not proud of it. Your father was gone, and Leo and

Evelyn had separated, although hardly anyone knew—she did everything she could to keep it quiet. He and I... Anyway, they decided to give it another try, for the boys."

"Wow, Mom," Mabel said faintly. Having an affair with a married man was unjustifiable, totally inexcusable—and yet Mabel's heart softened with sympathy. She knew all too well how it felt to love someone from a great distance, to feel powerless and rejected, to have your devotion thrown back in your face and for it to persist nonetheless.

"Ancient history now, but it's probably time you know the whole truth. None of us were innocent. Anyway." Norma sniffed, smiling shakily. "Maybe life threw you and Sam together again for a reason. This could be your opportunity to get it right, despite everything that went before. It is the season of second chances, after all."

"Maybe."

She tossed the word out casually, automatically, a way to close this exhausting conversation, to placate her mom's obvious need for hope that she hadn't ruined her daughter's romantic life forever. But as it left her mouth it solidified, took on the dimensions of something possible. Something real.

Maybe.

"Thank you for being honest with me," her mom murmured, scooping Mabel into a hug. "Everything will work out—I know it will. I love you."

"I love you, too, Mom." Mabel gave her mom a final

squeeze, then stood up.

"I'm going to grab some stuff from my room, and then I really need to get home. Early flight tomorrow."

"Of course, I almost forgot you've got a huge trip in the morning. Do what you need to do, and just shout if I can help."

"Will do," Mabel replied, and then cut across the small apartment to her childhood room, practically vibrating from the intensity of her exchange with her mom and desperate for the space to process what they'd just discussed.

She switched on the light in her closet, closed the door, and pressed her back against it. Of all the revelations tonight, the one throbbing most heavily in her mind was her mom's suggestion that she and Sam try again.

Ludicrous. The most far-fetched idea she'd heard in years.

Or was it?

She didn't actually need anything from in here, but she sat down and pulled out a plastic tub full of sweaters. She dug down to the bottom, where tucked inside an oversized cardigan she'd hidden a wide, wooden box long emptied of the puzzle pieces it once held. She slid off the top, her vision already blurring with tears.

The five years that changed her life, embodied in cards and pictures and hastily scrawled notes.

She couldn't remember the last time she'd opened the box. She'd even considered burning it all at one point.

Now she picked up the first photograph as gingerly as if it were a thousand years old, and might disintegrate if she wasn't careful.

Grainy, dark, and wildly unflattering, but her heart rate quickened nonetheless. A selfie taken on her first-ever smartphone and covertly printed at a drugstore kiosk. She'd held the camera too close, cutting out all but the barest hint of the background—a sliver of cinderblock, signaling one of Josh's many basement gatherings. Sam's face was turned to the side, his lips pressed to her cheek, the line of his jaw already breathtakingly masculine. She beamed into the lens, her grin so broad it squashed her eyes and gave her a double chin, her joy palpable, pure, and sublime.

She replaced the photo and held the box against her chest, letting her eyes fall shut.

Her mom was right—Sam was the only man who'd ever taken risks and made sacrifices for her and her alone. What if this was their second chance?

This trip would be their proving ground, she decided. She didn't know exactly where, or when, or how, but she'd find an opportunity and open her heart, lay it all out. Let him know how she still felt about him, and what she hoped they could build together.

Open the door, and pray he walked straight through it, toward her.

Mabel began to stuff the box back into the sweater—and stopped.

The truth was out now. No more skeletons in this closet. No more hiding from what was, or sulking over what could've been. The future was in her hands now, and she wouldn't let anyone interfere.

Mabel shoved the box onto a shelf, leaving it in plain sight for the first time in twelve years.

Then she shut off the light and stepped out of the closet, closing the door firmly behind her.

Chapter Ten

"I'M SORRY, SIR, they just booked the one room." The hotel staffer looked up with an apologetic wince. "And there's only one bed."

Sam exchanged a glance with Mabel, who shrugged in defeat.

"And there are no other rooms available?" he asked for the second time.

The woman behind the desk shook her head. "We're completely booked. Pharmaceutical convention."

That explained why the lobby was rammed with people in business attire wearing lanyards, but it didn't solve their problem.

"I could call the production team and see if they can move us to another hotel," Mabel suggested quietly.

Sam shifted his weight, propping his hip against the reception desk. He'd been on his feet more or less continuously since their plane landed in New York City that morning. Their rooms—or room, as it turned out—weren't ready so he and Mabel had taken to the streets, indulging every tourist whim her heart desired.

He'd had fun—more fun than he'd had in years—but hours of pounding the asphalt had taken its toll on his still-tender leg and spine, and the thought of waiting for another hotel to be arranged didn't appeal in the slightest.

He and Mabel could keep their hands to themselves for one night. Couldn't they?

"I'm okay with this if you are," he told Mabel. "At this point I just want to sit down."

"Same." She turned back to the staffer. "We'll take it."

Sam watched Mabel while she handled the particulars, unable to stop the endeared smile that crept over his mouth. Mabel was so confident and capable, it had delighted him endlessly to see her wandering around New York like the proverbial kid in a candy store, wide-eyed and slack-jawed.

After their crack-of-dawn flight they'd eaten breakfast in Central Park—bagels and coffee on a bench near Strawberry Fields, the autumn sky overhead bright blue and utterly cloudless. Then they'd wound their way down through the park, past the MoMA and Radio City Music Hall to Times Square, where he'd managed to keep his complaints to a minimum as they jostled with what felt like most of the rest of the population of the United States. They ate lunch in Bryant Park, inspected the lions in front of the New York Public Library, and then meandered east, toward the Chrysler Building.

"Isn't the UN over here?" Mabel had asked, and so Sam led her to the squat concrete building with its towering glass partner, the perimeter of the complex lined by flags.

"Damn, we missed the tour." She'd tapped on the printed schedule in the visitors' center.

"Not necessarily."

All the good he'd done in the world, the policies he'd influenced, the lives he'd saved, and yet nothing was as satisfying or filled him with as much pride as when he tugged his work ID out of his wallet and slid it across the desk to get Mabel a visitor's pass.

Some men had sleek VIP credit cards, or billfolds full of cash, or high-end sports cars to charm the women in their lives. He had credentials from a refugee agency, and as Mabel gaped up at the immensely high ceilings in the multistory lobby, he felt like the richest guy on earth.

Thankfully the building was quiet, so they were able to peek in at the vast General Assembly Hall, with its famous green-topped desks and gold backdrop, as well as the Security Council Chamber, where an enormous, multiscene painting loomed over the horseshoe-shaped table.

The drapes in the chamber had been left open, and they stood in front of the floor-to-ceiling windows overlooking the East River. Sunlight glinted on the chrome buildings on the opposite shore and sparkled on the intermittent peaks of the water. A unique and rare view of a picture-perfect New York City day—and he couldn't tear his gaze from the woman beside him.

"I used to hate coming here," he'd told her as they made

their way out to the plaza for a closer look at the river. "Being in these buildings meant I wasn't in the field. In fact, I think this is the first time I've been inside and not had to shake a single hand or kiss a single ass. Metaphorically speaking," he added.

"But it's so beautiful. Doing good work in such special surroundings—what a privilege. You've done all right for yourself, Sam Strauss."

The smile she turned on him rivalled the lights in Times Square.

"Thanks," he'd said quietly, before slipping his arm through hers. They took one last look at the river, and then by silent consensus they'd wheeled around and made their way toward the exit.

As the light dwindled they'd taken a winding path back to their hotel in Columbus Circle. Sam had been to the city so often it had become a chore instead of an adventure, but seeing New York through Mabel's eyes changed everything. Each ornate building façade was fascinating, every interesting-looking passerby a character brimming with backstory. Mabel brought everything to life around him, turning grubby, crowded sidewalks and tall, imposing buildings into a wondrous labyrinth of excitement and mystery.

She saw potential and worth wherever she looked. By the time they'd stopped for dinner, returned to their hotel, and stood waiting in the line at reception, he'd begun to wonder whether she could see potential and worth in him, too.

"And here are your key cards. Sorry again about the mix-up." The hotel staffer's voice reminded him where he was, and what lay ahead—an entire night crammed into a hotel room with Mabel.

"How are you holding up?" Mabel asked him as they rode the elevator to their floor.

"Not bad, considering, but I think I've hit the wall for the day."

"I dragged you all over," she said, apology in her tone as the elevator doors slid open and they made their way down the corridor. "You were such a champ, walking great, no complaints, I didn't even register how much distance we covered. Thanks for schlepping all over Manhattan with me."

"I had fun. If you'd asked me a few weeks ago whether I could've handled a day like this, I would've laughed. But you convinced me to stick with the rehab exercises, and they've helped a lot."

"I'm glad," she said simply, sliding the card in the lock and shoving open the door.

The lady at reception hadn't been kidding—there was only one bed. Big, but singular nonetheless.

For a moment they both stared at it, its implications deafening in the silent room.

But if Mabel wasn't opposed to the idea…did he have to be?

Something in him had shifted today as they'd walked

side by side. A kernel of an unfamiliar, uncomfortable emotion had taken root in his brain, and with every step it sprouted and grew, lengthening and strengthening until it had taken firm hold of his thoughts.

Doubt.

You'll ruin her life like I ruined your mother's. For twelve long years he'd taken his father's words that fateful night in August as gospel. Not lightly, or without scrutiny, or because it was the first and only time his father had ever been so honest with him, but because as much as it wounded him to acknowledge it, they had the ring of truth.

He'd witnessed more violence and trauma than anyone should, and yet his nightmares were of Mabel, naked and vulnerable, wrenched out of his grip and ushered away, her eyes wide and scared and brimming with tears as she glanced back at him over her shoulder. He'd never felt so powerless, or as much of a failure as he did that night, unable to help her, unable to save her from whatever horror lay ahead.

Alone with his dad, predawn light glowing at the edges of the curtains, the reality he'd been refusing to face finally landed squarely in his lap. In a matter of days he'd be gone, nearly a thousand miles away from the wrath she wouldn't be able to escape, the humiliation when word of their discovery spread, the whispers, the disapproving glances.

I could stay, he'd thought, and then immediately, *No, I can't.*

That was the moment he knew his father was right. He

was too flawed, too selfish, too undeserving of her devotion. He was sorry for what Mabel would endure, but not to the extent that he would spend even one extra night in his awful, too-quiet house, caught between his mother's seething, impotent indignation and his father's weary, self-pitying defeat.

And so he'd left. Left Mabel, left Orchard Hill, left the version of himself who was allowed to get close to other people, to imagine permanency, to pretend he wasn't doomed to repeat his father's mistakes.

But what if he'd been wrong?

He shoved his overnight bag in the corner and dropped onto the edge of the bed, leaning down to unlace his shoes and kick them off. Then he lay flat on his back, staring up at the textured, white ceiling, willing the sudden ease in his muscles to spread up to his gnarled thoughts.

Mabel flopped down beside him, propping her chin on her hand. She smiled, and he knew instantly, heavily, as certainly as he knew his own name that she was the future he wanted—if he could convince himself he was the future she deserved.

"We're in the middle of New York City," she told him. "World-class nightclubs, famous restaurants, probably more bars than St. Louis has people. We've missed the Broadway curtain times, but we can do almost anything else. What do you feel like?"

He grinned. "Want to watch some Danish guy solve a

murder?"

OF ALL THE ways Mabel had ever dreamed she might spend a night in New York City, watching a moody, subtitled Scandinavian drama on a tablet hadn't featured.

Now that she was here, though, she wouldn't have it any other way.

"Don't tell me he's following this guy into a pitch-black warehouse without calling for backup." She rolled her eyes, reaching into the bag of M&Ms she'd bought in the airport and popping a few in her mouth.

"His partner was right there—do they not have walkie-talkies? Shouldn't he at least give him a heads-up that he's chasing the killer?"

"But then they couldn't have a dramatic, one-on-one showdown."

Sam narrowed his eyes at her in mock accusation. "Have you seen this already? No spoilers."

"Just a hunch, but who knows. Maybe the killer will drop his knife and turn himself in, apologizing profusely for the truly extensive amount of police time he's wasted."

"Or the detective simply gives up, and the killer lives happily ever after in the fjords."

"We'll see. I need to stop eating these." She leaned forward again, picked up the bag of M&Ms, and stretched across Sam's extended legs to deposit it on his side of the bed. When she eased back against her propped-up pillows she'd inadvertently closed the distance between them on the bed. Now their hips bumped, their ribs barely an inch apart.

She didn't move over.

Neither did he.

This had been on the cards since the moment the woman behind the reception desk said there was only one bed. She knew it; he knew it.

She was ready. Unbeknownst to him, this whole day had been a sort-of job interview for the rest of her life. Her mom's words echoed in her head, the suggestion that she and Sam might try again, the revelation that even though in the end he left her, he'd risked more to love her than anyone else.

For someone who had no idea he was being evaluated for long-term relationship potential, Sam's performance was pitch-perfect. When she grumbled about their predawn flight time, he'd settled her in a chair and gotten them both big coffees. She could tell some of the more touristy parts of their day hadn't thrilled him, but he'd been good-humored and patient, agreeing to even the cheesiest photo ops. And when he'd whipped out his badge and escorted her straight into the United freaking Nations, she'd practically passed out right there in the lobby.

Tonight she didn't want to think about the miles between Finland and Missouri, or the career that kept him out of the country for months at a time, or Ellie's ominous warning, or her guilt at abandoning her no-chasing resolution almost as soon as it went into effect.

Because she wasn't abandoning it—she was reframing it. This was the start of a year she intended to live selfishly, finally putting herself first, letting life bring her what she wanted instead of wasting her energy running after it. Life had brought her Sam Strauss, and she needed to know whether this was a second chance—or a long goodbye.

Their conversation dwindled as the show ended, their awareness of each other muffling the dramatic conclusion on the screen.

Sam stretched his arm along the upper edge of the pillows—a silent invitation. She accepted, snuggling against his side. He curled his arm around her, his hand resting on the top of her thigh.

Mabel smiled into his cotton shirt, remembering their first date. They were in seventh grade, at the movie theater with a group of friends. About fifteen minutes in Sam had tentatively slipped his arm around her shoulders—the middle-school equivalent of an engagement ring. She'd grinned in the darkness, tilting toward him, giving him her tacit approval.

By the end of the movie her neck ached and her shoulders burned and the plastic armrest dug into her side, but she didn't care. Sam Strauss was her boyfriend, and life was perfect.

One night, she reminded herself. No heavy thoughts, no looking back.

Sam had undone the top three buttons of his shirt when they'd arrived in their hotel room, and despite the shadows she could make out the light spread of hair across his chest, the same cognac brown as his head. That expanse of skin had been boyishly smooth the last time she'd touched it, and she wondered how else his body had changed.

He smelled amazing, like the welcome, earthy freshness of stepping into the sudden shade of a wooded section of trail on a hot hike. His arm was solid and strong around her waist, and her body awakened with the gradual, scattered cadence of lights coming on in windows at twilight.

Sam felt it, too. She sensed the growing tension in his arm, the slight uptick in the heartbeat she could just make out, and his unnatural stillness, as if he was afraid to do anything to disrupt this moment of perfect, unspoken connection.

Neither of them spoke as the credits rolled. Finally, even those were over, and Sam released her, killing the screen on the tablet and moving it to the bedside table.

For a second she braced herself, wondering if she had this all wrong. Waiting for Sam to swing his legs over the side of the bed to put space between them. To tell her this was a bad idea, that they were borrowing trouble, and this would only make it hurt more in the long run.

Instead he resumed his seat and held out his hand, gesturing for her to come closer. He tugged her more tightly against his side, his hand rising to tease the ends of her hair.

"Mabel, I—"

"You don't need to say anything," she interrupted. They'd talked plenty these last couple of weeks. Time for their instincts to take over.

Whether it turned out to be a wonderful idea or a catastrophic one, they were going to make love tonight. She couldn't think of a single word in the English language that would change that.

Still, she sensed his hesitation.

She pulled out of his grip and sat up straight, looking him in the eyes.

"We're adults, Sam. We're not hurting anyone."

"Except each other."

"You won't hurt me," she promised, and hoped to God it was true. That her heart would be intact if they went their separate ways when this was over.

"I'd never forgive myself if I did."

The hoarse intensity in his voice pushed her off her sure emotional footing and for an instant she stumbled, her thoughts flailing until she managed to regain her grip on the certainty that had gotten her to this point in the first place.

If he's meant to love me, he will.

That was her New Year's resolution. To wait, holding her heart in reserve, until love chose her.

But what if he doesn't? Because you're already falling—

"I know you have to leave," she told him, blurting the first words that came to her mouth in a desperate effort to silence that unwelcome, unhelpful voice deep inside her mind.

She reached up to touch his cheek, the faint stubble rasping against her finger, immersing herself in this moment—in his scent, his presence. "I have my New Year's resolution, remember? The love of my life is going to walk straight toward me, and I won't spare a glance for anyone else. I won't be hurt when you go. Not this time."

He flinched and she pressed closer, regretting that clumsy reference to the moment twelve years ago, which seemed less and less important.

"I want to enjoy you, Sam—enjoy us, the way we should've been. We'll deal with tomorrow when it dawns. But tonight let's be together."

He studied her, his expression uncertain, before his mouth curved in a hesitant smile.

"Where do we start?"

"Here," she said, and kissed him.

He responded instantly, encouraging her, allaying whatever lingering concerns she had that he wasn't one hundred percent on board. His hands moved to her lower back and she flung one leg over his knee, sliding her palms up his chest.

Their adolescent romance had been a slow burn, both of them such risk-averse, rule-following Goody Two-Shoes that they'd clung to their virginities until their senior-year prom. Their group of prom-goers had rented a couple of cabins at a campground in Granite City, and for one special, blissful night they took advantage of finally having a bedroom to themselves.

Sometimes, as she'd lain beside her now ex-husband, listening to the snoring she coached herself she'd get used to eventually, she relived that night in her mind. At the time she felt like a horrible, unfaithful person for doing it—but now that she knew he'd been literally having sex outside their marriage, she wished she'd saved the guilt.

In high school she'd tried to keep her expectations low, had read countless magazine articles and blog posts about how it was okay for the first time to be awkward, and even to feel sore. She'd smiled encouragingly at Sam in the darkened cabin bedroom, simultaneously bracing herself for discomfort and pain.

But he'd been so careful, so attentive, easing inside, his blue-gray eyes fixed on hers until arousal overcame him and he squeezed them shut, making a strangled, self-restrained sound that even now made her thighs clench.

He'd be different now. He already was, kissing her with greater dominance than he ever had then, his tongue moving with confidence and hunger, his hand slipping down to squeeze her backside. She liked it—liked it a lot—yet at the same time she couldn't help smiling against his mouth, remembering that earnest young man in the dusty cabin, and the way his inexperienced, utterly sincere body had made her own sing and shudder and practically split open with pleasure.

"What's funny?" he murmured.

"Just thinking about that cabin in Granite City."

"And that makes you laugh, huh?"

She shook her head, running her fingers through the hair over his temple. "You were very sweet."

"I was so nervous."

"Are you nervous now?"

"A little. For different reasons."

"Don't be." She gave him the same encouraging smile from over a decade ago. "We're grown-ups. We can do this."

"I think you might've said that in Granite City, too."

"And I was exactly correct." She pressed a sweet, swift kiss on his lips.

"I'll never forget the way you looked at me that night," he told her softly, running his thumb over her lips, across her jawline, down her neck. "Excited, a little apprehensive, but most of all, I remember your trust. I knew you had total faith in me, and to this day I've never felt so honored."

"You earned it. No one's ever loved me as completely as you did, Sam. Not even my own father."

"Mabel," he said roughly, the two syllables practically bursting with anguish and affection and something so very close to exactly what she wanted that it thrilled and terrified her in equal measure.

He reached between them and squeezed her hand. Then he dropped it and opened his arms.

"Come here."

The hint of a sultry growl in his voice, the glimmer in his eyes—she scrambled into his lap. He repositioned her legs so she straddled him, flashed her one of his boyish, heart-clenching smiles, and then brought his mouth to hers, picking up where they'd left off.

God, the man could kiss. Funny to think she'd been spoiled for life by an inexperienced teenager. Then again, she supposed it made sense, since for years their marathon make-out sessions were as far as they'd gone.

She squirmed in his lap, reliving those hot, heavy interludes, usually in the darkened corner of someone's basement or the back row of a movie theater, anywhere they could steal time and evade discovery. Having this whole night together felt incredibly luxurious by comparison, and her pulse beat faster, impatience threatening at the edge of her mind.

Sam, on the other hand, was in no hurry. He kissed her thoroughly but leisurely, tangling his fingers in her hair, slipping his other hand beneath the hem of her shirt to trace lazy shapes along her lower back. He tasted like chocolate and caramel and something even sweeter, a flavor uniquely his own that she hadn't realized she'd hungered after until she'd recognized it again after so many years.

She tried to stay in the moment, to relax and savor him, but her need thrummed with increasing urgency. She began unbuttoning his shirt, reminding herself they had all night. She could quench her dry, burning thirst quickly, and then come back for seconds.

And thirds, and fourths…

She pushed the light-blue cotton off his shoulders and leaned back, admiring the view as she ran her hands down his chest. He was broader now, raw-bodied and hard, less gym-built than in his high-school swim-team days, and yet somehow far sexier. His gaze never left her face, his smile bemused when she dragged her own up to meet it.

"Your turn," he said.

Mabel gripped the hem of her long-sleeved shirt, hesitating for only a moment as she considered the fifteen pounds she'd put on since high school, then tugged it over her head and tossed it on the floor. If he was looking for someone with the body of an eighteen-year-old, well, he'd just have to—

"Damn," he breathed, in the enthralled, incredulous tone of someone who'd just seen a famous painting in person for the first time.

The insistent, sudden way he yanked her to him, by contrast, was not the etiquette of someone visiting the Louvre.

She threw her head back as he worked his mouth over her throat, her collarbone, down to the hollow between her breasts. His breath was warm against her skin, and as she dug her fingers in his hair the heat pooling between her legs turned molten, fiery and insistent and increasingly desperate.

She reached between them and undid his jeans, then slid her hand inside and squeezed the steely length she found there. Sam groaned, throbbing against her palm.

That was all the incentive she needed. Mabel scrambled off his lap and began hastily undressing, unzipping her jeans and sliding them down her legs. Sam stood and followed her lead—although she spotted his covert, self-conscious glance her way as he slipped the last bit of denim over his injured leg, revealing the still-fresh, red scar that slashed across his shin.

Mabel closed the distance between them and draped an arm around his waist, pressing her other palm in the center of his broad, hard chest. She pushed up on her tiptoes to kiss him and he obligingly lowered his head, his mouth easily finding hers.

"I don't care about your scar, or how you walk, or anything stupid and superficial like that," she whispered, her lips barely a breath from his. "I—"

She caught herself just in time, the word *love* dangerously and unexpectedly close to leaping off her tongue.

"I want you exactly as you are," she managed, inwardly reeling from her near-miss.

She gave herself a little shake. This could still all go sour. There were no guarantees they'd even see each other again after this trip. She was prepared to give him a second chance if he wanted one—but the keyword was *if*.

Hold it together, she coached herself.

Then she slipped her hand into his boxers and squeezed his hot, tight ass.

He growled into her hair and dragged her down to the bed, pressing her onto her back. He kissed her neck as he slid his hands behind her and fumbled with the clasp on her bra, eventually lifting his head enough to tilt her to one side and frown at the tiny, stubborn hooks.

"You were bad at this in high school, too," she teased, reaching back and unhooking it in a single, one-handed motion.

"I'm out of practice." He tugged the straps down her arms, flung away the offending scrap of nude-colored fabric, and cupped both of her breasts, exhaling reverently.

Mabel let her head fall back on the bed as he palmed her bare flesh. He circled his thumbs over her nipples, then replaced each one with his tongue in an alternating rhythm of sucking and stroking that had her clamping her thighs together, trying to contain the feverish heat that ignited there and was rapidly spreading across her body.

Sam was warm and heavy on top of her, and when he shifted slightly his erection dug into her thigh, big and hard and tenting his cotton boxers.

Feeling the extent of his arousal filled her with impatience, and she tugged on his hair, pulling his head up from her breasts to look up at her.

His gaze was dreamy, his eyes half-lidded, and he blinked several times before he focused on her.

"Get a condom," she instructed.

His eyes widened, his expression turning desolate. "I don't have any."

She arched a brow, and he sprang up off the bed, already reaching for his jeans. "There's a drug store on the corner. I'll be back in ten minutes."

"Your lack of optimism surprises me, Sam, but you're in luck. I've delivered enough babies produced from exactly this sort of scenario to always carry contraception. Check the zippered pocket on the inside of my purse."

He practically threw himself across the room, where he pulled the strip of foil-wrapped condoms from her bag with the look of a man who'd struck gold. He stripped off his boxers and set to work opening one of the packets, apparently oblivious to the effect the sight of his thick, rigid cock was having on the woman waiting on the bed.

Mabel yanked down her panties, which by now were soaked through. She scooted up to prop herself on the pillows and licked her lips, her fingers itching to slip between her legs, to relieve some of the urgency built up at her core, but she resisted. She wanted to save everything for Sam, and give him every last piece of herself.

Because she'd already given him her heart, she finally admitted as he returned to the bed and eased on top of her, smoothing his thumb over her lips. For all her big talk and no-strings ambitions and so-called resolutions, she'd fallen for him, hard, and no matter what she might tell herself, she knew then and there it would hurt like hell when he left.

If he left.

He smiled, and for a second he was the boy she'd known, the floppy-haired, sweet-voiced young man who loved her, who had yet to abandon her.

This is your second chance, she told him silently, parting her legs, opening her heart.

He reached between them and touched her, arousal clouding his gaze as he found her slickness, rubbed it up and over her clit, and then slipped one finger inside.

"Do you want this?" he asked, his eyes locked on hers.

She nodded.

"I need to hear you say it."

"Yes, Sam. Yes."

He sank into her with a groan and she clutched him tightly, her back arching with pleasure at the delicious intrusion, the tantalizing fullness.

He held still, his breathing ragged, and when she looked up at him the adoration in his face brought a lump to her throat.

This was it—this was as complete as she'd ever felt, and maybe ever would. For better or worse, Sam was the love of her life.

The question was whether he felt the same.

"Sam," she gasped, the word hoarse and choked.

"I know," he murmured, his smile soothing and sincere. "It'll be okay."

And just like she had that night in the grimy cabin in Granite City, she trusted him. Wholly, easily, without question or second-guessing.

She loved him, she believed him, and she had utter faith that he'd make the right choice for them both.

He kissed her, deeply and with intent, and then began to move within her. His hips set a smooth rhythm and she followed, meeting his thrusts, each collision ramping up the scorching need throbbing at her core.

Despite her attempts to hold it off, her orgasm crept closer and closer, until she felt like she was tiptoeing to the edge of a volcano and then leaning over, until the heat from the roiling lava licked her face and warmed her cheeks. She sensed Sam's tension, felt the muscles in his arms quivering with restraint, and from the way he watched her, dragging himself from being hyperalert to her reactions before slipping again into slack-jawed bliss, she knew he was close.

His disintegrating control threw her own into jeopardy, and then it was gone. She moaned, her thighs trembling, her fingers clawing at his shoulders as she put one foot over the edge of the volcano, and pushed up on the toes of the other.

And down into the fiery depths she fell.

Sam tumbled after her, but she barely noticed as her body exploded in a blaze of white-hot light, somehow simultaneously splitting her apart and making her utterly whole, more seamlessly complete than she'd ever been before.

She wasn't sure how much time she lay peacefully under Sam's weight and warmth, languid, boneless, and deeply satisfied, trailing her fingers along his back. Eventually he rolled off, gingerly removed the condom and threw it in the trash, and then resettled beside her, urging her onto her side so he could spoon her from behind.

"That was fun," she said lightly, and then smiled as his deep chuckle resonated against her back.

"An understatement and a challenge in three words. Nicely done."

She sighed happily, lacing her fingers through his where they rested against her stomach. There would be plenty for her to process this encounter, but for now she closed her eyes, content to doze in the strong, capable arms of the man beside her.

"Mabel?"

"Hm?"

"Can I tell you something?"

He sounded serious. She yawned, trying to shake off the drowsiness that had been about to consume her. Then she rolled over so they were facing each other, their heads on their respective pillows.

"Is it the kind of something I should get dressed for? It's hard to feel authoritative in an argument if my boobs are everywhere."

"We're not going to have an argument, and your boobs, if somewhat distracting, are perfect."

"Then proceed."

For a minute he simply looked at her, his expression thoughtful, as if he was planning exactly what to say.

"It's about that night in August," he told her finally.

Inwardly she cringed, hoping it didn't show on her face. Did it always have to be about that night? Couldn't they finally put it behind them?

But he clearly had more to exorcise, so she nodded for him to go on.

"After they found us, after my dad took you home… I was up all night with my parents. My mom was furious, my dad was silent, I had no idea what happened to you, if you were all right—I've never felt so powerless, before or since. I didn't protect you, and I should have."

"We were eighteen years old, Sam, with no money or means. We didn't even have our own cars. What more could you have done?"

She reached across to stroke his face, but he stopped her, lacing his fingers through hers and lowering their folded hands to the space between them on the mattress.

"It's not that, it's… Remember what I told you, the next day? That I didn't want a relationship?"

"Of course I remember."

"It wasn't an excuse, and I didn't lie to you. I truly meant it."

Her heart was in her throat. "Do you still?"

"I don't know," he said, his face taut and anxious.

"Where did it come from? Because you'd never said anything like that before."

"I think that's what I'm trying to tell you." He smiled weakly. "My mom ranted at me for hours that night, as you can probably imagine, but it all bounced off. I had no regrets, and I was so confident it'd all work out. Yes, it would be hard to be away from you, but we'd make it work. I loved you. Nothing else mattered."

She swallowed hard, blinking back the tears burning against her lids at the acknowledgment that they'd been so close to happiness, so nearly spared from all this pain. "And then?"

"My mom went to bed around dawn. My dad stayed. He'd barely said a word all night, but there was something about the way he sat on the edge of my bed, staring at his hands—I'd never seen him so serious, and it scared me to death."

Sam inhaled, looking past her to that night twelve years ago, and she tried to imagine it, too. The shaky weariness of a night with too much adrenaline and not enough sleep. The late-summer sun rising bright and hot. The birds cheerfully chirping in the tree on the other side of the window, oblivious to the grave scene within.

He refocused on her with a sad smile. He squeezed her hand, then released it to trail his index finger down her cheek.

"He told me to let you go. He said if I didn't, I'd ruin

your life like he ruined my mother's."

"And you believed him?" she asked, incredulous—but the answer was in his eyes.

"After watching you being ripped away from me, and realizing I wasn't selfless enough to stay in Orchard Hill to be with you instead of leaving for college, knowing you would take all the heat while I escaped, I thought maybe I already had."

"I know your dad stayed to be with your mom, but I would've never asked you to do that. If anything, I wanted to find a way to go with you."

"That's exactly my point—he should've left, like I did." Sam flipped onto his back, rubbing his hand over his eyes. "My mom would've been brokenhearted for a while, and then she would've found someone else and moved on. Instead they stayed together, their devotion became resentment, and they were miserable for their entire marriage. My dad wasn't cut out for a relationship, and neither is my brother—that's why he's still alone. Maybe I'm not, either."

Mabel propped herself up on her elbows. "Wait, you think the problem is your dad was just ill-suited to being with someone for the long term, and that's why your parents were unhappy? That it's, what, a genetic condition or something?"

"No—that I have the same personality, and the same selfish predispositions that would make history repeat itself. Choosing a woman whose devotion is unwavering and unmatched. Doggedly committing to her, failing to measure up, and then refusing to admit defeat until I've destroyed both our happiness."

"But that's exactly what you did, only it wasn't a relationship you clung to past its expiration date—it was this idea that you don't deserve one."

"I didn't say that I won't ever deserve a relationship, just that—"

"You have some inherited ability to screw it up?" She rolled her eyes, sitting upright. "Come on, Sam, you're smarter than that. You convinced yourself that I'd be better off without you. How is that not self-pitying? If you truly believed you were worthy of my love, you would've fought for it, not blamed yourself for a future that hadn't even happened—and probably never would have."

"But doesn't that prove I wasn't worthy?" he asked pointedly, pushing up beside her. "If I was stronger, better, somehow more capable, I wouldn't have lost you."

"First, you told me this wouldn't be an argument," Mabel grumbled, snapping up his discarded shirt from the floor and buttoning it over her breasts. "Second, you didn't lose me. I'm right here. And I'll give you another chance, if you ask for it."

She couldn't quite believe she'd just said that, and judging from Sam's blinking, slack-jawed expression, neither could he.

It was there between them now. She lifted her chin and

set her mouth. Her heart might be beating wildly, she might feel like her whole life hung on what he decided to do next, but she could at least look brave, dammit.

"Mabel, I don't—I didn't think—" He stopped, looked down at the floor, raised his gaze back to hers, and tried again. "I never want to hurt you again," he said softly.

She didn't understand what he meant, other than it wasn't what she wanted to hear, and she stuffed her devastation behind a wall of annoyance.

"For God's sake, Sam, your dad is not an authority on relationship success. He and my mom had an affair."

His eyes widened. "What did you say?"

"My mom told me last night. I should've said something sooner, but everything was going so well, I didn't want to rake up old graves."

"When? For how long?"

"I don't know any details—I probably don't want to. He and your mom were separated, but then he decided to go back to her for your and your brother's sake. That's all she said."

Sam muttered a string of profanities as he stood up and rapidly got dressed, yanking a new shirt out of his overnight bag.

"Wait, what are you doing? We're in the middle of talking," she said, the last few words rising on a borderline plaintive whine.

"I have to go, but I'll be back. We'll finish this, just not right now."

"No, Sam," she commanded, suddenly overflowing with anger, barely stopping short of stomping her foot. "I don't know where the hell you think you're going, but—"

"My dad lives in Connecticut," he muttered. "I have to talk to him."

"Then call him."

"It's not far."

"It's the middle of the night, and we're going on national television first thing in the morning," she practically shouted, working hard to keep the hysteria out of her voice. "You can't possibly be serious."

He didn't respond, but his silence was confirmation enough.

"You'll never get back in time."

"I will."

She shook her head, incredulity and rage and abject despair tightening her chest and weakening her legs. She wanted to shake him, to scream in his face, to do whatever it took to keep him here beside her.

"Seeing your dad won't make a shred of difference to us or our lives. What our parents did, who they were, it doesn't matter. It's over, it's done, but I'm *right here*."

Her voice broke on the last syllable, and frustrated, helpless tears spilled onto her cheeks. Sam paused long enough to shoot her a conflicted look, but then pulled on his socks and began to tie his shoes.

"This is something I have to do. I can't be who you deserve until it's finished." His voice was deadpan, his expression determined. Mabel began to sob openly, her hope and optimism and fleeting chance at joy slipping out of her reach, draining out of her heart.

Sam straightened, tugged on his jacket, shouldered his bag, and then wrapped his arms around her.

"Don't walk out on me again. Don't let their mistakes kill our happiness," she whispered into his chest.

He held her for so long, saying nothing, his grip tight and steady, that for an instant she thought he might've changed his mind.

Then he kissed the top of her head and murmured, "I'll come back. I promise."

He let her go.

And then he left.

"God*damn* you," Mabel roared, reached for the nearest object to hand—her sneaker, as it turned out—and flung it against the closed door. It bounced off and landed on the floor, leaving door and shoe unharmed.

It didn't bring Sam back, either.

Mabel collapsed on the bed, dropping her head in her hands.

She wept for Sam, for the damage done to him by his parents all those years ago, and for the loneliness and isolation he'd put himself through without any good reason.

She wept for herself, for the disintegration of what felt

like her last chance at love, for her failure to guard her heart once again, and for the long road of healing that lay ahead.

Mostly she wept for what should've been their shared future, and would now be lost to the ages. She'd hoped they could escape the past, but tonight it dragged Sam away from her again—and for the last time.

She'd given him his second chance, and instead of walking toward her, he'd run away. This would hurt—this would hurt more than anything she'd ever done—but she had to accept that they were over for good. Time to honor her resolution, honor herself, and do what she needed to move on.

Mabel dried her eyes on the sleeve of his shirt. Then she took it off and stuffed it in the trash, stepping into her own pajamas instead. She took out her phone and blocked Sam everywhere she could—social media, email, and good old-fashioned voice calls. Once that was done she fired off an email to the production crew, asking if she could please be moved to a different flight home.

Then she shut off the light, slid between the sheets, and cried herself into a drained, dreamless, utterly heartbroken sleep.

Chapter Eleven

ONLY A HUNDRED miles separated Sam from his father's home in Middletown, Connecticut, but it turned out that even in the city that never sleeps, public transportation occasionally took a nap.

If it hadn't taken so much energy to arrange the trip, if the urgency and complexity of the task hadn't fed the problem-solving instinct left famished by his sabbatical, maybe he would've slowed down, stepped back, and realized this was a dumb idea. That whatever he needed to settle with his father could wait, and the woman who'd just opened her heart to him could not.

Or maybe he was simply afraid. Afraid of the power of his feelings for Mabel, the lack of control they implied, and the potential for his life to be turned completely upside down—and researching train and bus timetables was a hell of a lot less scary than being head over heels in love.

Either way, he threw himself into the task single-mindedly, and after concluding that a bus-and-train combination wouldn't get him to Middletown until eight o'clock the next morning—when he needed to be back for the taping at ten—he took a rideshare to a twenty-four-hour car rental agency. He slid his credit card across the counter and was soon behind the wheel, heading north out of Manhattan.

The road was nearly empty, and as the glittering lights of New York City gave way to dim, repetitive highway, the thoughts he'd been able to hold at bay with his determined exodus rushed into his mind.

He had a lot to unpack in his exchange with Mabel, but right now he only had interest in two of the facts clamoring for his attention: his dad cheated on his mom, and Mabel had offered him a second chance.

No—the second was too big, too overwhelming to even begin to consider before he'd dealt with the first. He couldn't face the future until he and his father got right with their overlapping pasts.

He reached the two-bedroom, single-story house just after three o'clock in the morning. He'd only been here once before, to help his dad move in after the family home was sold in the divorce, and he squinted at the neighboring houses, realizing he had no idea who lived in any of them. He felt displaced and intrusive, the anonymous, darkened windows and the unknown families within them an alienating contrast to the weeks he'd just spent in Orchard Hill, where he knew at least one person behind more than half of the front doors in town.

He'd always assumed his parents' sudden move from Missouri to Connecticut had been about him, that leaving for college finally liberated them to fly the empty nest, get distance from the past, and start over somewhere new. Of course his dad said it was about the job, the promotion, but as Sam shivered in the wee-hours cold he wondered for the first time if it was his mom's plan. With no kids at home to tie them together, maybe she was worried his dad would leave for good.

The recollection of his father's infidelity reignited the anger that had pushed him to this point in the first place, and he pounded on the door, each stinging strike of his fist more satisfying than the last.

A light came on in one of the front windows and the door swung open.

"Sam? What are you doing here?"

In plaid pajama pants and a white T-shirt, squinting from the doorway, Leo looked smaller and slimmer than Sam remembered. For an instant he felt ridiculous, driving up here in the middle of the night, banging on the door.

Then he reminded himself of that fateful utterance twelve years ago. The decade of his life he'd spent alone, refusing to get close to anyone. Mabel pleading with him to stay—and his decision that this had to be done first.

"We need to talk," Sam said tersely, and shoved past his father into the house.

"Is everything okay? I thought you were in Orchard Hill."

"I was in New York. With Mabel."

"Is she all right?"

"No. Neither of us have been all right for a long time, and you, and Mom, and Norma need to answer for that."

Leo scrubbed his hand over his eyes and motioned to the worn, peach-colored couch that had once inhabited their basement in Orchard Hill.

"Have a seat. I'll make coffee."

Sam took in the room around him while his father was in the kitchen. His dad had approached the splitting of household assets with an air of preemptive defeat, and so all the furniture was second best. The unloved couch was flanked by the scratched, wobbly side table from the spare bedroom, and the flat-screen TV on which the volume wouldn't go above twelve was mounted above the flimsy, chipped unit with a drawer that never quite closed.

The walls and surfaces were bare—no photos, no art, not even a fresh coat of paint to suggest that whoever lived here intended to stay. In fact everything Sam could see of the living room, adjacent dining room, and opening to the kitchen was unlived-in and impersonal. The whole house had a temporary feel, as if it were a short-term rental, and not the home of a man with a career and a life and two grown children.

Sam shifted, discomfited by his surroundings—because they were so familiar.

Everywhere he'd been, all the rare and special places he'd visited, and he, too, lived between empty walls. For years he'd told himself his sterile, minimally furnished apartment in DC was a reflection of his busy travel schedule, but as he leaned forward on that old, basement-dwelling couch he knew this was his future. Isolated, alone, with little evidence that he'd ever meant anything to anyone, and only his regrets for company.

Remarkable to think that his dad had tried to urge him onto a different path, and succeeded only in ensuring that Sam followed in every one of his footsteps.

That changed tonight, Sam resolved as his dad returned with two cups of coffee. Sam accepted one and Leo lowered himself into a fake-leather recliner with a broken footrest.

The coffee tasted strong and bitter, and Sam thought the milk might be expired. He nodded to the theme park logo on the side of the mug as he placed it on the side table.

"Mom didn't fight you for this treasured souvenir, huh?"

"I think that was an outing she was happy to forget."

Leo's rueful smile echoed his own as he recalled that long, hot, slog of a day. Something had been simmering between his parents all morning and erupted over lunch. He and his brother had sat in front of their empty hot-dog wrappers for what must've been an hour, quiet, stony-faced, while their parents bickered in hissing half whispers. Eventually Leo and Evelyn had lapsed into angry silence, and spent the rest of the afternoon irritably shuffling their children on and off the rides, glaring at each other whenever they had the chance.

"You screwed up, Dad," Sam told him flatly.

Sam assumed his father would object. That Leo would deflect at least part of the blame on his mother.

But when Leo nodded, sadly, slowly, Sam realized he barely knew the man across from him at all.

"There's a lot I should've done differently," Leo agreed. "But there's clearly something specific on your mind, and I'm assuming it has to do with Mabel Antonoff."

"She's the catalyst, but the issue sits squarely between you and me. Do you remember what you said to me that night before I left for college? After you found Mabel and me together, after Mom laid into me for hours."

"I told you to let her go," his dad said softly.

"Because I would ruin her life like you ruined Mom's."

For a minute neither of them spoke. The echoes of that long-ago exchange reverberated through the room, so palpable it was practically a third party to this conversation, perching on the edge of the sofa, head cocked, curious but largely dispassionate about the havoc it had caused.

"This isn't what you want to hear, but I was right. If anything I'm more certain now than I was then."

Sam gaped at his father. "What did you say?"

"I'm sorry, Sam, but you two were on a one-way road to heartbreak. You were young and naïve and asking each other for a level of long-distance commitment that's unsustainable even for most adults."

"We would've made it work," Sam interjected, but Leo

waved his hand in dismissal.

"The distance was only part of it. Mostly it was… I saw the devotion in her eyes, Sam. If you hadn't ended it then, it would've only gotten harder, and eventually you would've broken her heart beyond repair. I know it was difficult, but you were better off alone."

"I wasn't—I'm not. I'm miserable." The word tumbled out, plaintive and desperate, and Sam dropped his elbows to his knees, bowed by the weight of his confession.

"I didn't tell you to be single forever," Leo snapped. "Not every relationship has to be Romeo and Juliet. Look at your brother, he's not married and he—"

"Zach is married to work," Sam shot back.

"And so were you until very recently."

"Things change," he muttered.

"You think I don't know that?" Leo demanded, leaning forward in his chair. "I tried to spare you what I went through with your mother, and if you want to hate me for it, I can't stop you—but I won't apologize. Mabel would've pulled you back to Orchard Hill and you had bigger, better things on your horizon. Your love would've become guilt, and then resentment, by which point you'd be out of alternatives."

"Who exactly are we talking about, Dad? Because this story sounds familiar, and it's not mine."

"It would've been, if I hadn't—"

Leo broke off suddenly, rubbing his fingers over his eyes

before leaning back in the recliner.

"I don't want to fight with you, Sam. I thought I was protecting you from making a huge mistake. Clearly you disagree."

Sam shook his head vehemently. "This is not an agree-to-disagree situation, Dad. You interfered in my life, told me I would *ruin* the life of the woman I loved. That affected me for years. It still affects me today."

"You could've ignored me."

Sam stared at his father, jaw slack in disbelief. "Is that the best you've got?"

Leo threw up his hands. "What do you want from me? You show up in the middle of the night, arguing about something I said a million years ago. Did you expect me to have a speech prepared?"

"Norma Antonoff apologized to me."

Leo jerked upright. "She what?"

"She said she was sorry. That the three of you shouldn't have made it so hard for us."

"She's right. She usually is." Leo sighed wearily, and the fight visibly drained out of him. He looked suddenly older, as if he'd aged ten years in ten seconds.

"It's hard for me to hear that I hurt you, when my intention was to help. I looked at you and Mabel and I saw me and your mom. Maybe that was unfair—"

"It was."

"Then I'm sorry. I genuinely believed that over time

you'd fall out of love with Mabel and feel too guilty about it to leave her. Like I did."

"Except that's not quite the full story, is it," Sam said carefully. "Mom could be clingy and needy, sure, and she didn't always make life easy, but you had something else to be guilty about. You had an affair with Norma."

The color faded from his father's face. "Who told you that?"

"Norma told Mabel."

"It's the worst thing I've ever done," Leo said hoarsely. "That, and the car accident with your mother, when we were in high school. I really messed up both their lives, didn't I?"

Sam didn't speak. The wretchedness in his father's voice cut him deeply, more sharply than he expected, but it wasn't his place to absolve him. Leo needed to seek forgiveness from other quarters, Sam realized, and his own dispute seemed a lot more minor in comparison.

"I guess I messed up yours, too. I really am sorry, Sam. I thought I was doing the right thing. I thought you'd be better off alone."

"Thank you for the apology," Sam replied softly. He saw the suffering in Leo's expression, and his righteous indignation and seething fury and persistent impulse to blame his father for more than a decade of anguish ebbed away until it vanished.

His dad had enough to atone for. Sam had aired his grievance, and now he would let his father take it off the list.

"And thank you for hearing me out. Especially at this somewhat unsocial hour." Sam smiled weakly, and his father returned it.

"I know that ultimately I'm the one responsible for what happened between me and Mabel. I could've ignored you, I could've defied you, I could've done a thousand things differently. At the same time, I needed you to know you were wrong, and you shouldn't have said what you did. You and Mom weren't helpless, cosmic victims of a failed marriage. You both made choices—choices I wouldn't have repeated, if given the chance."

"You mean the affair."

Sam nodded. "I know Mom played her part, but you had to know that being unfaithful wouldn't fix anything. I never cheated on Mabel—I never did anything except love her. So your comparison, and your prophecy of doom were a little unfair."

"You're right. What can I say—you're absolutely right. And if it's any consolation, I'll regret what I said for a long time."

"That's no consolation, actually. I needed to have this conversation, to revisit that night one more time. Now I'm done. Ready to move on. And you should be, too."

Leo's smile was bitter. "Easier said than done, but if you want me to, I'll try. Does this mean you and Mabel are reconnecting? I know you were doing this little press tour, but—"

"I'm in love with her."

That truth revealed itself calmly, without fanfare, matter-of-fact and quietly indisputable. To his surprise Sam wasn't scared, or nervous, or even mildly astonished. On the contrary, his love for Mabel felt like something he'd known for a long time, a fact so undeniable and inescapable that it slipped into his subconscious, a constant but unacknowledged presence, like remembering to breathe.

"I hope she gives you another chance."

"I hope so, too," he replied, but even as he heard the confidence in his words he recalled their argument in the hotel room, her pleas for him to forget the past and remain in the present, his own stubborn, blinkered refusal to listen, to deviate from this vital mission he'd told himself couldn't wait another minute.

Maybe he'd been right. He felt almost reborn, having finally gotten this twelve-year-old weight off his chest. He felt whole, and strong, and ready—ready to be the man she deserved.

Yet he couldn't shake a burgeoning sense of uncertainty.

Had he made a terrible mistake—again?

"Anyway, I should get back to the city. We're filming our last TV appearance in the morning."

"Are you sure? You just got here, it's the middle of the night, and that's a lot of driving on no sleep."

"Thanks, Dad, but I'm sure."

"Grab a power nap in the guest room before you go, at

least. You'll be no good to Mabel wrapped around a telephone pole."

"I'll be fine. I promise."

"Shmuel," Leo said sternly, the use of Sam's Hebrew name snapping him to attention exactly as it had done for thirty years. "I want you to be safe behind the wheel. Have a nap, and then you can go."

He supposed his dad had a point—and they'd both already been victims of traumatic, life-changing car accidents. It was just after four—he could sleep for a couple of hours and still be on his way in plenty of time to make the taping.

"All right—you win. That bed better have clean sheets."

Leo followed him to the second bedroom, where a thin mattress reclined on a lopsided box spring, but the sheets—if faded and pilled—smelled like fresh laundry.

The mere sight of it sent a wave of sleepiness crashing over him, and Sam yawned.

Just an hour or two, and then he'd be on his way.

"Thanks again for the talk, and taking me in at three o'clock in the morning," he said as Leo began to leave the room.

"You're always welcome, wherever I am. And thank you for the honesty, and for giving me the opportunity to try to make it right."

"You did."

Leo ducked his head, stepped out of the room, and then leaned back in, his hand on the knob.

"Norma... Did she get remarried?"

Sam shook his head. "She's single. Actually, she asked me for your number."

His dad's expression moved from surprised to thoughtful. "Well. Goodnight, Sam."

"'Night, Dad."

Sam stripped off his shoes and jeans and stretched out on the bed. He unlocked the screen on his phone and hastily tapped out a text to Mabel.

Sorry I ran off like that. All fixed now, glad I did it, will be back in the morning. So much to tell you, and I can't wait to see you. Sweet dreams.

He hit send and silenced his phone, placing it facedown on the floor beside the bed. Then he crossed his arms behind his head and smiled into the darkness.

He'd made peace with his father. He was in love with Mabel. Tomorrow he'd tell her. Tomorrow his life would change for good.

Everything was finally falling into place.

Sam closed his eyes and fell instantly asleep.

"ARE YOU SURE you don't want to give him five more minutes? Or try his phone one more time? Paige is still in makeup, so we're not in a rush."

Mabel caught the producer's eye in the mirror and shook her head. "Sam had a family emergency. He won't be here."

The producer's mouth twisted sympathetically, and she reached forward to squeeze Mabel's shoulder.

"You're going to be amazing. Paige can't wait to talk to you. Anything you need, just let me know."

"Thanks," Mabel told her sincerely, and then turned back to the face in the mirror.

Today would be a hard day. That's what she'd been telling herself since shortly before she finally fell asleep, sometime around two o'clock in the morning, and again as soon as she woke up. She'd repeated that mantra as she showered, packed up, checked out of the hotel, and took a taxi to the TV studio.

She didn't even try to find magic in the fact that she was in an honest-to-God yellow taxi, or gape at the photos of celebrities plastered around the studio's walls, or enjoy being pampered by the unbelievably friendly and helpful producers, stylists, and makeup artists. She knew that anything resembling happiness would be a bridge too far.

Today she had to focus on survival.

In the hours before she'd finally stumbled into a restless, ragged sleep, her thoughts had bounced like a pinball between doubt, anger, and resignation, in more or less that order. She wondered whether she was overreacting; raged at Sam for making such a stupid choice and putting her in this position; and then comforted herself that she was just back to the beginning, really. Sam had been out of her life for twelve years, and until a few weeks ago she had no expectation otherwise. That he'd reappeared, that they'd reconnected, that she'd fallen in love with him—in retrospect that was always bound to be a detour from the long road to happiness. More fool her for not seeing it earlier.

No matter what she told herself, or how she imagined this situation might play out differently, one fact remained clear: she asked him to stay, and he left. Not to attend a family emergency, or anything even close—although she counseled herself that barring a true disaster, his reason was immaterial.

He'd left. Again.

That was that.

She'd braced herself for a confrontation when he returned, except the hours ticked past, and there was no sign of him. Her hypothetical fantasy of what she would say when she saw him again shifted settings several times, from the hotel to the lobby, from the lobby to the taxi, and most dreadfully, from the taxi to the TV studio. In the end it was pure fiction, more wasted time and energy, because he didn't come back at all.

She worried briefly that he might be in trouble, had been in a car accident or something and couldn't reach her because she'd blocked his number—and then threw that concern away like so much trash. His dad lived near enough, and if he were in a hospital—God forbid—someone there could get hold of her.

No, there was no good excuse for his disappearance, but

perhaps no surprise in it, either. Twelve years ago he ran out on her, and her limitless, naïve love for him. Of course he'd do the same now.

"We're ready for you." The producer stood in the doorway, smiling encouragingly, a clipboard held to her chest.

"You look gorgeous, if I do say so myself. Knock 'em dead, girl." The makeup artist who'd so kindly and discreetly set to work fixing Mabel's puffy, been-crying-all-night face grinned, spinning the chair around.

Mabel thanked her profusely, then followed the producer down the hall to the set.

She turned the corner just in time to see a man in a headset remove one of the chairs from the stage. Her lower lip trembled, and it took everything she had not to ruin every drop of her sympathetically applied makeup.

But then she stepped all the way into the set and saw the studio audience. Rows and rows of predominantly women, all of whom turned their heads to look at her when she entered—and then burst into a round of applause.

"Yeah, midwives!" someone shouted from the far end of the room, and now Mabel's makeup was really under threat. She called a thank-you with a wave, and then walked to the stage, her chin a little higher.

As she took her place on the tall chair and settled her skirt over her thighs, she exhaled, letting go of a nagging concern she hadn't wanted to articulate to herself until now.

She hated to admit it, but she'd been worried the show

would cancel altogether when they found out Sam wasn't coming. He was the one who gallivanted around the world, saving lives. She did what thousands of other midwives did every day, and other than happening to be in a hardware store at the right time, she wasn't any more remarkable than the rest of them.

Except that she was here, and she had this opportunity. She'd do her best to make the most of it.

The audience warm-up guy got everyone applauding, and then he introduced Paige Harris, who entered with a wave from the other side of the stage. Mabel sat patiently while they filmed an opening piece with Paige standing in front of the show's logo, discussing the themes of the upcoming episode. Then they stopped for a commercial break and Paige walked over, taking the seat across from Mabel's.

"I'm so glad we get to talk today," she said, leaning over to squeeze Mabel's hand. Paige was in her midfifties, with a tidy, gray bob, and a smile much warmer and more sincere than Mabel expected.

"Thank you for having me."

"It's my pleasure! I gather we've lost your companion to a family emergency. I hope everything's okay."

Mabel nodded, carefully keeping the lid on that can of worms. "I'm sure it will be."

"Since you and I will have a little extra time, would you be comfortable talking about your divorce, and your approach to relationships now that you're single again? So many of our viewers find themselves unexpectedly on their own after their marriages break up, and it would be great for them to hear from someone as confident and resilient as you are."

Mabel fought the urge to glance over her shoulder to see if Paige meant someone else. *Confident* and *resilient* were the last two words she'd use to describe herself in this moment.

But what could she say? *Actually, I completely lost my mind over my ex-boyfriend and now he's abandoned me a second time, so I might not be in a good position to give advice.*

No—just like this was her opportunity to represent midwifery, so too would she represent the brokenhearted. She'd made a good resolution. She hadn't stuck to it, but she'd had the right idea. That's what she'd focus on. Not the past mistakes—the future.

"I wouldn't consider my life a romantic success story, but I'm happy to share what I can," she told Paige.

Paige brushed off her comment with a wave. "Trust me, no one watches this show to hear about easy roads to happiness. Our viewers have been bumping up and down in potholes for years, they've got the dents to prove it, and they want to know they're not alone."

"Then they've come to the right place."

Paige winked, and then turned to the camera. "When we talk about superheroes, most of us probably imagine people with amazing powers, like flying, or mind-reading, or becoming invisible. But what about the real-life superheroes who walk among us? They may not have glittery capes or high-tech command centers, but they're just as extraordinary. My first guest today rose to viral fame after delivering a baby in a hardware store with the help of none other than the high-school ex-boyfriend she hadn't seen in over a decade. Here to share her story of everyday heroism is Mabel Antonoff."

The audience erupted in a fresh round of enthusiastic applause, and Mabel felt her cheeks go hot.

You can do this, she coached herself. *You* are *doing this.*

Once the cheering died down Paige continued, "Take us back to that day in the hardware store. You're there, just shopping for garden supplies or whatever—"

"Wall hooks, to hang pictures."

"Wall hooks," Paige echoed with a grin. "You've got décor on your mind, prepping for some decorative DIY, and then what?"

Mabel recounted the story of the birth, including the shock of realizing her erstwhile assistant was her former high-school flame. Her throat tightened momentarily at the memory, and the knowledge of how that particular story had ended, but she thought about all the people who tuned in to this show for hope and inspiration, and she held it together.

Paige transitioned into asking her about midwifery—how she'd chosen it, what motivated her—and as Mabel answered she knew she'd hit her stride. The previous interviews had perfected her ability to articulate her thoughts on the subject, to avoid rambling or being tangential, and to emphasize her core points: choice, safety, and support.

"So it's not really about whether you want an epidural or not, it's that you're armed with information, options, and a team that supports whatever decision you make," she concluded, and the audience exploded into clapping, cheering, and even a whistle or two.

Paige held her hand over her heart until the applause died down, and then she said, "I know I'm not the only person here wondering where the heck you were when I was pregnant."

Mabel smiled graciously as more applause rang around the studio. "I haven't mastered time travel quite yet, but midwifery is becoming more and more available all over the US. I'm working on expanding my own program in St. Louis. I'd encourage anyone considering pregnancy to at least meet a midwife and see if it's a good fit."

"Wonderful advice. Thank you, Mabel," Paige said earnestly, and then turned to the camera. "Mabel and her ex-boyfriend captured the nation's imagination, as social media speculated wildly on the potential for a romantic reunion. How does it feel to have the whole world weighing in on your love life? When we come back, Mabel has more for us on her divorce, *that* ex-boyfriend, and what's next on her journey.

"That was fabulous," Paige told her as a makeup artist

jogged over to sweep powder over the host's cheeks.

"Thank you." Mabel beamed. She had the same sense of self-congratulatory buoyance as when she'd aced a test or gotten praise from a teacher. She'd nailed that segment, and even if she blew the next one, she'd walk away happy with a job well done.

But she wouldn't screw up the next one, she assured herself. Just because she'd been wildly unsuccessful in relationships didn't mean she had nothing to offer. She'd learned more than her share of hard lessons, and maybe she could help someone else—or at least show her fellow heartbroken singletons that they weren't alone.

She *was* heartbroken, she acknowledged, swallowing a thick lump. But she wasn't hopeless, and she sure as hell wasn't giving up.

"We're back with my guest, midwife and viral sensation Mabel Antonoff," Paige said into the camera as filming resumed. "Mabel's viral moment came not only from her everyday heroism and professional calm, but from her unlikely assistant when she delivered a baby in a hardware store. Mabel, there was so much speculation around the two of you, and I know a lot of us were hoping for a reunion that ended in a romantic happily-ever-after. Did it?"

"It did not," Mabel replied with what she hoped was a brave smile.

"Were you hoping otherwise?"

Mabel took a deep breath. She had two choices. She

could shrug this off, offer a polite, vague reply, and insist that she and Sam were better as friends and planned to remain that way. No one could fault that response, and she could walk away from these fifteen minutes of fame knowing she'd been gracious and honorable.

Or she could tell the truth.

She glanced at the audience. Most of the faces she saw were women; many were middle-aged or older, past the twentysomething phase at which there seems to be endless time for flirtation and butterflies and first dates. There came a point when life gained a certain heft, a level of complexity that made relationships more significant, less flimsy, no longer dime-a-dozen and disposable. Somewhere along the line she'd crossed that threshold, and she knew how bleak the view could be on the other side.

Would it be so bad to plant a flag in that daunting landscape? To add a spot of color, a sign of life, a reminder to whoever came upon it that they weren't the first, and they weren't the only.

Sam was gone, and her media moment was running its course this very instant.

Might as well go out with a bang.

"Being completely honest, I was," she admitted. "He was my first love, and our breakup was awful. He left me then, and I thought that if he came back, maybe someone else important would, too."

"Who's that?" Paige asked gently.

Mabel smiled, but it wasn't enough. Her eyes brimmed, and the two words came out shaky and thin. "My dad."

She blew out a slow breath, trying to collect herself, as Paige passed over a tissue. Mabel dabbed at her eyes and cleared her throat, careful not to look at the audience. A chorus of sympathetic sniffles popped up around the room, and she knew if she saw someone else in tears, there'd be no cleaning up her own emotional mess.

"My father left when I was really young," she continued, proud of how clear and calm she sounded. "So young that by the time I was a teenager, I barely thought about him. He moved on right away, had another family, sent a card for the first couple of birthdays and then gave up."

Paige winced. "I'm sorry."

Mabel lifted a shoulder. "For most of my life I told myself it wasn't a big deal. How could I care about someone I barely knew? Then Sam and I got together, and then he left me. I had other boyfriends—they all left me. I got married, and guess what?"

"He left, too," Paige supplied.

"Of course he did." Several tongues clucked in collective disapproval of her ex-husband.

"So after years of being walked out on and left behind, I decided it was time for a change. We've just passed Rosh Hashanah—that's the Jewish New Year—and I made a resolution. No more chasing love. If the right man exists, and he's out there, he'll walk straight toward me."

Paige sighed. "I love that."

"Too bad I didn't stick to it," Mabel remarked with a roll of her eyes, prompting chuckles from the audience. "When Sam reappeared, I thought maybe it was a sign. In the end it proved to be more of a test, and I failed. I let myself believe that he'd been the one who'd broken my heart in the first place, so he also had the power to heal it. But that wasn't fair to him, and it wasn't truthful, either. He wasn't my first heartbreak—that was my dad. And until I reckon with that part of my past, and understand that my father's abandonment doesn't mean I'm not worth keeping, I'm better off on my own."

Mabel sat back in her chair as the audience applauded firmly, not entirely sure where that had all come from, yet found herself believing every last word.

It was as if taking a step outside herself and seeing her story through the audience's eyes made it all clear. Her mom was right. Her dad left her first, long before she met Sam. What could Sam have done, then or now, to heal that wound when she refused even to name it until right this moment?

Of course it still enraged her that Sam walked out last night, choosing to right an old wrong instead of opting in to the happiness in front of him—but maybe he'd done them both a favor. She owed her past a closer look, too.

Anyway, it was over now—all of it. Her brush with fame, her even more fleeting fantasy of a future with Sam. Time to turn toward the future for real, to focus on her career and herself and her community and her journey to being wholehearted and strong.

As the clapping died down, Paige reached across the space between their chairs and squeezed Mabel's hand.

"Thank you so much for sharing your story with us. I know there are people here right now who feel the same." She turned to the audience. "Who else knows the abandonment of a parent?"

Loads of hands shot up.

"I want to hear how it's shaped you, and your ability to form healthy, trusting relationships." Paige accepted a handheld microphone from one of the assistants and moved out to the audience in a typical component of her show.

Mabel nodded along with the audience members' stories of absent fathers and cheating husbands, and put her hands together for their subsequent tales of reinvention, whether nascent or complete. Then Paige thanked her again, and looked into the camera to set up the next segment after the commercial break. Filming ended.

She was done. Hollow, still a little devastated, but ready to move forward.

Or so she thought.

Mabel began to slide down from her chair but a producer stopped her, stepping in closely.

"Sam is here," she said in a low voice.

Mabel's breath caught in her chest. She could see Paige

eyeing her, but the host didn't interfere.

"Has he been listening?"

The producer nodded.

Mortification flashed hot in her cheeks, but then she remembered this was going to be on network television—and that there was no shame in honesty or vulnerability.

"Would you like me to bring him out? We could extend your segment to talk to both of you. Who knows, maybe Paige will help you two get to a resolution after all."

For one wild, reckless moment she actually let herself believe it might be possible. That Paige could say something they hadn't said to each other, or hadn't said to themselves, that would change everything. That would erase the past, and the pain, and the terrible blunders they'd both made, and finally give her the man she'd always wanted.

Then reality resettled heavily on her shoulders, and Mabel wished she had nearly as much hope in her heart as the producer had in her voice. The truth was she and Sam had their chance, not once, but twice. She had to commit to everything she'd said, and not just because an entire viewing audience heard it. She owed it to herself, and to him, to protect them both from making this awful mistake a third time.

"No," she replied, politely and firmly.

Disappointment was visible on the producer's face, but she didn't argue. "Would you like to see him backstage? Otherwise I can put you in a separate room."

"No, thank you. We've said all we need to say to each other."

Every word was like plunging her hand into a fire and holding it there, yet she managed to smile.

"If you're sure," the producer said slowly.

"I'm sure."

Mabel and Paige exchanged a hug and a thank-you, and with one last wave to the audience she followed the producer offstage and back to the green room where she'd been waiting earlier. She avoided glancing at the closed doors in the corridor, knowing Sam was behind one of them, painfully aware of how easy it would be to choose him, to bridge those inches and satisfy her short-term desire—only to pay for it in the long run.

Again.

Mabel sighed, packing up the few things she'd taken out of her purse and sweeping the room to make sure she wasn't leaving anything behind. She wished things were different. She wished she and Sam were in a position to hug and make promises and leave hand in hand, but they weren't.

He left her twelve years ago; he left her last night. She couldn't expect him to change so fundamentally that he wouldn't leave her again. That was her work to do now.

To love herself enough to stop chasing him—really stop, this time—and wait for the man who was truly meant for her to find her instead.

She hiked her bag up on her shoulder and took one last

look around the room, at the city glittering outside the window, and at this magical, semifamous world she'd inhabited for a brief time. The last few weeks had been a fantasy she couldn't have dreamed up in her deepest sleep. The media attention, the opportunity to share her story and her passion for her profession, and the growing promise of a future with the man she'd never quite let go.

But like all dreams, it had to end.

She shut the door on the green room, and on this chapter of her life. Then she started toward the exit, her eyes wide open.

Chapter Twelve

SAM PROPPED HIS elbows on the back of the empty pew in front of him and dropped his face into his palms. The sky outside Temple Sinai was almost fully dark, and the restless anticipation of his fellow worshippers was palpable. The end of their twenty-five-hour fast for Yom Kippur was nigh, but he wasn't ready. Not even close.

Decades ago, in Hebrew school, he'd been taught that ancient temples remained unlocked as long as the sun shone. That's why the last service of the Yom Kippur holiday was called Neilah, the Hebrew word for *locking*. As the light dwindled, so too did this once-a-year opportunity for atonement, and for an unparalleled period of closeness to God in which anything was possible. Soon the gate would shut, and Sam would be on the outside again, left with whatever version of himself remained.

He wasn't sure what he'd expected when he'd risen at dawn, ignored his already gnawing hunger, donned his yarmulke and taken a seat in the synagogue. A divine roadmap, maybe? A voice in his ear, outlining exactly how to repair the life he'd so spectacularly screwed up in only a couple of days? A whispered suggestion of what the hell to do next?

Since high school Sam had been single-mindedly focused on one plan or another, pushing toward his goals with barely a glance to either side. The trip to New York had changed that completely. He was adrift, with no idea what tomorrow would or should bring, and he didn't like it.

The morning of the taping had been an unfunny comedy of errors, but even then he'd retained his focus, kept his eye on the prize. He'd overslept, gotten stuck in impenetrable traffic, and of course discovered that Mabel had blocked his phone number—yet he'd persevered. He was an expert in catastrophe, literally a professional navigator of disaster, so he kept calm, stayed patient, and when he eventually arrived at the studio he was level-headed and unflustered despite his chaotic journey.

Then he heard Mabel speak, and his whole world fell apart.

Through every slow, stressful mile between his dad's house and the studio he'd imagined the happy reunion that awaited them. He'd apologize for leaving the night before and she'd grudgingly forgive him, understanding that he'd needed to make peace with his dad. He'd promise her happiness, tell her he loved her, and swear never to leave her again. She'd believe him, see his sincerity, and confess that she loved him, too. They'd kiss, and hold each other, and everything would be perfect.

Admittedly he hadn't made a plan for what happened next, and in the end it didn't matter. She hadn't forgiven him—she wouldn't even speak to him. And what he heard her say to the audience devastated him.

Of course she was worth keeping. He hated that she believed otherwise on any level, hated that her father's abandonment made her feel unlovable, hated that he'd continued the pattern, hated that he'd perpetuated this toxic myth that no man would choose her forever.

He loved her beyond comprehension. He was desperate to tell her. But he had no idea how.

His options were also in short supply. He had an offer on his grandparents' house, a seat on a flight to DC the day after tomorrow, and another ticket booked to Helsinki two days after that—but the last thing he wanted to do now was run.

Sam was desperate to talk to Mabel, to try to put this right. Even if she rejected him, at least he'd know he'd done all he could, and shown her every honest, broken, unrelenting piece of himself. Except short of turning up on her doorstep—which seemed intrusive and disrespectful, given the effort she'd put into blocking his contact—he had no idea how to go about it.

He supposed that was part of what he'd come to synagogue in search of—a way back. To the woman he loved, to the man he could've and should've been for her all those years ago.

Funny to think that's why he'd returned to Orchard Hill

in the first place. He thought he wanted to reconnect with the young man he'd been, full of drive and determination and passion.

He never suspected that he was actually looking for the woman who'd made him that best version of himself.

"*Shema Yisrael Adonai Elohenu, Adonai echad.*" Rabbi Spellman's voice broke through his consciousness, tugging him up from his slumped-forward position.

"*Baruch shem kevod malchuto le'olam va'ed,*" the congregation echoed, and then again, and again, for three repetitions in total. Nighttime thickened outside and Sam clenched the edge of the pew in front, panic rising in his chest.

The gate was closing, but he wasn't ready. He didn't know what to do.

God, tell me what to do.

"*Adonai Hu Ha'Elohim.*" The phrase echoed around the sanctuary once, twice, seven times, each collective iteration stronger and firmer than the one before as the congregants almost embodied the divine unity they exhorted. Their gathered voices were ardent, solid, resolved—the exact opposite of his own, rapidly splintering coherence.

"No," he murmured under his breath as the cantor raised the shofar and took a deep breath. *Not yet*, he begged, dropping his head back onto his hands and squeezing his eyes shut.

The horn sounded. Yom Kippur was over.

The gate was closed.

Sam didn't move. He heard the shuffling of belongings against polished wooden pews, the trickle and then steady stream of footsteps toward the door, and the muffled voices that quickly became cheerful and congratulatory as the solemnity of the occasion gave way to the joy of breaking a fast. He kept still, waiting for the sanctuary to empty, straining his ears in the fresh silence, an absurd, last-ditch effort at receiving divine guidance.

Instead he heard the brush of cloth on the pew next to him, and the faint creak of wood as someone settled comfortably into the space beside him.

Reluctantly he opened his eyes, glanced to the side, and had to search his memory to put a name to the familiar face.

"Jonah?" he whispered.

The rabbi's son nodded, smiling a greeting.

"You okay?" he asked, his voice hushed.

"Fine," Sam replied, but the word emerged laced with so much misery he knew Jonah didn't believe him.

Jonah looked contemplative for a moment, then inclined his head toward the door at the back of the sanctuary.

"Let's get something to eat."

The only thing worse than wallowing in his own wretchedness would be trying to hide it while making small talk in a room full of starving congregants. He shook his head.

"Meet me in the little kids' classroom. I'll bring the food. Five minutes." Jonah's tone was surprisingly firm. He slapped Sam's back companionably and walked out.

Sam hesitated, lingering to soak up just a few more seconds of this unique state of suspension, this once-a-year opportunity to dig deep, look hard at your failings, and resolve to do better. Then he got stiffly to his feet, wincing at the ache in his back from hours perched on the wooden pew, and left the sanctuary.

A few minutes later Sam flicked on the light in the classroom, which seemed a lot smaller than when he'd been here as a child, singing songs and learning the *aleph-bet*. The chairs had certainly shrunk, and as he lowered himself with great difficulty onto a tiny plastic stool, praying it didn't break, he wondered why on earth Jonah had specified meeting here—and why he seemed insistent on meeting at all.

As if summoned by Sam's speculation, the door opened and then shut behind the rabbi's son—and Ellie's boyfriend, Sam reminded himself. Ellie still hadn't warmed to his reappearance like the rest of his high-school friends, but Jonah's friendly smile as he set down a loaded paper plate suggested he didn't share his girlfriend's animosity.

"Is there a reason we're meeting in Munchkinland?" Sam accepted the water bottle Jonah offered, gulping down half of it as Jonah made his equally awkward journey down to the tiny chair.

"I figured no one would find us this far down the hall, but to be fair, I didn't consider the furniture."

"I'd suggest we move but I'm not sure I can get up."

"Me, neither. Let's eat, so at least we'll have the strength to call for help."

Jonah picked up a slice of quiche and popped it in his mouth, but Sam eyed the food warily. He was so hungry his hands were shaking, yet he felt unworthy. Like he deserved just a little more suffering.

Jonah's gaze moved from his face to the food and back again. "Do you want something different? I can go back."

Sam shook his head. "No, this is great. I'm just not sure I earned it."

Jonah studied him for a few seconds, and when he smiled, it was kind. "Did you know I went to rabbinical school?"

"No, Mabel told me you were an EMT."

"I am now. I dropped out before I was ordained."

Sam's attention snapped up. "Really? But your dad is—"

"The rabbi. And yes, he was extremely angry and disappointed. We're working on it, though."

"Good for you. I have some history with my dad, too. Hard to realize they weren't always the men we wanted them to be."

"I'd drink to that, if I had anything stronger than water. Anyway, on the off chance my failed career as a rabbi gives me any credibility, I like to think that fasting isn't about punishment, or achievement, or not being good enough. It's a conduit—not a test. And in my experience, the day's reflections are better processed on a full stomach."

Sam lifted a shoulder, still a little uncertain, but he supposed Jonah had a point. He picked up half of a sesame bagel with cream cheese and lox and took a bite.

"Better?"

Sam nodded, and Jonah grinned.

"So, tell me about your Yom Kippur," the rabbi's son urged, angling his legs away from the squat table between them to stretch them out. "It doesn't seem to have left you with much peace or fulfillment."

"Is it that obvious?"

"I don't know if you remember, but I was in the ambulance crew that arrived after the baby was born," Jonah said, politely evading the question.

"Vaguely." Sam squinted, trying to recall the specifics of that strange and significant afternoon.

"Doesn't matter. My point is only that I've been watching your story unfold, maybe a little more closely than Ellie—who is firmly Team Mabel, but I think you know that."

"I do, and I don't mind. I'm glad Mabel has such a loyal friend."

"She is that." Jonah smiled, distractedly, affectionately, and jealousy seared through Sam's chest. He so badly wanted Mabel to smile that way about him, but that seemed more fantastical than ever.

"I heard the trip to New York didn't end well."

Sam waited for Jonah to continue, but instead he popped a raspberry rugelach in his mouth, giving Sam plenty of patient silence.

"I screwed it up," Sam admitted finally. "Again."

Jonah kept quiet, and Sam found himself gratefully filling the space, the words tumbling over each other.

"We had an awesome day, and then we slept together, which wasn't the problem, but we were both feeling vulnerable and sharing a lot of truth and she told me something I didn't know, something from a long time ago that didn't change the way I felt about her at all, something about my dad, and I wanted to deal with it right away, so I left. She asked me not to, said it didn't matter, and she was right—it could've waited, and I made everything worse. So much worse. But I wanted to come back to her with a clear heart, and I thought I couldn't do that if I didn't do this other thing first. I wanted to get rid of all that old baggage so that when I told her I loved her, she was just getting me, and nothing else—no bad history, no heavy past. Except she didn't see that. She just saw a man leaving her, again, like her dad, like her ex-husband, like I did. Now she won't talk to me, and I have no idea what the hell to do."

Seemingly unfazed by the verbal tidal wave that had just washed over him, Jonah said simply, "That's rough."

"Yeah." Sam put down his half-eaten bagel, his stomach suddenly too tight with worry and dismay to take another bite.

"I came to synagogue this morning hoping for a burning-bush-type revelation. I thought if I concentrated, and silenced all the noise in my mind, and truly tried to get closer to God, I might figure out how to fix this. Sounds ridiculous, huh?" Sam offered a sheepish smile.

"Not at all—it was a good idea. And you probably did get your answer, just not as clearly as you expected."

"What do you mean?"

"We don't all get a burning bush, but God has a way of making Himself known." Jonah leaned back as much as the tiny chair allowed. "What crossed your mind while you were in shul today? What did you think about?"

"Mabel," Sam answered promptly. "How much I love her, and how stupid I am for losing her again."

Jonah nodded for him to go on. Sam exhaled, parsing through the hours and hours he'd spent in that pew.

"I thought about this place—Orchard Hill. Why I left, and why I'm here now. Who I used to be here. How this community shaped me. And whether I waited too long to come home. How much I've changed, and if any of it can be undone."

"And?"

Sam shrugged. "I don't know."

"Sure you do."

Sam peered quizzically at Jonah, who was the picture of unhurried serenity, his expression even and attentive, his fingers laced over his stomach.

Shame he'd given up on the whole spiritual counselor thing. He would've been damn good at it.

"I did think about how I miss being part of somewhere, like I was here. My home life was pretty crappy so I spent a lot of time around town, at school, and here, at Temple Sinai. It's cheesy, but I miss just *knowing* people. This community isn't perfect, and it hasn't always been kind to Mabel or her mom, but I had my own slice of it, and it was where I belonged. I haven't felt anything like that since."

Jonah's eyes were narrowed in thought, and after a few moments' contemplation he asked, "Could that be your answer?"

Sam frowned. "Could what be my answer?"

"This community. Your connections. Who you were here, and who you want to be now."

"I don't follow."

"You said you left Mabel in New York so you could come back without baggage. But that backfired, right?"

"Right," Sam said cautiously.

"Maybe it's okay to carry a little weight from our past, especially if it informs who we are, and improves who we'll become. You already confronted the ugly side in New York, and you'll do the work to reconcile with it. In the meantime, maybe this is your chance to reach back again—not to fix anything, but to get a little support. That safety net may not have fallen as far as you think."

That sounded way too good to be true, and Sam opened

his mouth to argue, then closed it again.

What if Jonah was right? He'd wanted so badly to come home to Orchard Hill and rediscover himself so he could move on and build a life like the one he'd had here. But what if that old life was still within reach? What if there was just enough forgiveness and loyalty and bone-deep friendship left to get him to exactly where he wanted to be? And what if *he* was still enough of his long-ago self to deserve it?

He couldn't quite believe it, but he wanted to. He so desperately wanted to.

"All right, then tell me." He raised his chin, looking Jonah squarely in the eye. "What's your plan?"

> *I'm going to have a great life, Dad. I'm going to fall in love with a man who'll never leave me, and we're going to be happy for the rest of our days. I would love for you to be a part of that, but if you don't want to respond to this email, or if you'd prefer not to have any contact in the future, I understand. I just want you to know that I forgive you, and I love you.*

Mabel wrote her name at the bottom of the email, and although her finger hovered over the button to send it, she opted to save it as a draft instead.

She would sleep on it, she decided, shutting her laptop and setting it on the coffee table. This letter was decades in the making—no need to rush it, especially on the heels of a twenty-five-hour fast. She'd get a good night's sleep, eat a healthy breakfast, and then take a second look.

"In the meantime, doughnuts," she announced to the empty room.

She went to the kitchen and opened the box of brightly frosted, sprinkle-dusted doughnuts she'd bought for a breakfast treat. She'd already polished off two, so when she placed the third on a plate she also picked up a knife to cut it in half—and then put it back down.

"I earned this," she muttered, carrying the plate and the undisturbed doughnut back to the couch.

Damn right she had. On the surface everything was going fantastically well. She'd barely landed in St. Louis when she got a call from Cathy Lopez on behalf of the hospital's steering committee.

"Sorry for bothering you on your day off, but I thought you'd want this news as soon as possible. We just approved your proposal to roll out the midwifery program across the system. I already sent the staff requisition to the recruiting team. We are full steam ahead, Mabel, and the credit goes entirely to you."

She popped a piece of doughnut into her mouth, smiling as she thought back over that conversation, and the series of congratulatory calls from other senior leaders that had followed. She couldn't remember ever receiving such a flood of positive feedback, and while she wished her plans and ideas had been taken more seriously *before* she found herself on TV addressing a national audience, she was grateful.

Her relationship with her mom was also stronger than

ever. Norma picked her up from the airport and they had a long, honest discussion that carried on until it was so late, Mabel ended up spending the night in her old bedroom. More and more she empathized with the young woman her mother had been, the scale of her heartbreak, and the difficult decisions she'd faced. Would she have done better in the same circumstances? Maybe—maybe not. Either way, truth only brought them closer, and Mabel intended to keep it that way.

When sunset marked the commencement of Yom Kippur, Mabel had locked her apartment door and silenced her phone, programming a single exception for the hospital in case the midwife on duty was overwhelmed and she needed help. Then she lit a scented candle, sat down with a notebook, and began drafting a letter to her father.

The end product was probably only a few hundred words long, but it took her the majority of the twenty-five hours to compose and what felt like twenty-five years to emotionally process. The time spent in her own head, acknowledging where she could have done better, forgiving herself, and recognizing that sometimes it simply wasn't her fault, was draining but surprisingly healing. When she finally put her hands on the laptop keyboard Yom Kippur was nearly over, and it took her until after sundown to finish, but she felt a lot better.

Whether or not her father responded, whether this changed anything in her day-to-day relationship with him—

or lack thereof—seemed less important now. She'd done the work, interrogated the way his absence had colored her self-perception and her choices, and when her scented candle burned out, a line of smoke drifting up from its spent wick, she felt steadier and more confident than she had since the day Sam left her.

The first time.

Mabel sighed, polished off the doughnut, and reached for her water glass.

Despite all the areas in which her life had been unburdened these last few days—her job, her mom, her long-absent father—her heart was heavy. She was cheerful with her mom, professionally upbeat with the stakeholders at the hospital, and her email to her dad was remarkably calm and diplomatic. But she was grieving, and she didn't want to admit it to anyone.

She loved Sam. He was gone. And she wasn't sure how she could get over him.

Funny to think that when it came to processing her father's abandonment, recognizing how she'd internalized his gradual disappearance from her life, and finally trusting that she deserved better, her heart and mind were totally aligned.

When it came to Sam, however, they couldn't be farther apart.

She knew perfectly well that she should move on, find someone new, and put that inconstant, impossible man behind her.

But, dammit, she didn't want to.

He was just so…perfect. All she'd ever wanted in a partner. Smart, funny, sexy as hell. Considered, respectful, yet rock-solid in his ethics and values. He was the only man with whom she'd felt like a genuine half of a whole, sharing ideas and power and trust in seamless balance.

Why couldn't he see that? Why did he have to keep ruining everything?

Tears brimmed and she blinked them back, shooting up from the sofa and hurrying away from this line of thinking.

She set her plate next to the box of doughnuts—the night was young, she might have a fourth—and then realized she still hadn't checked her phone since the holiday ended. She unplugged it from the charger and unlocked the screen for the first time in more than twenty-five hours.

A few days after the initial viral onslaught she'd completely disabled her social-media notifications, but she had a bunch of emails, a few texts, and weirdly, several missed calls from Ellie in the last half hour.

She tapped Ellie's number to call her back. Her friend picked up on the first ring.

"Hey, how was your fast?"

"Really good—so good I'm a little late getting back to my phone. Is everything okay? I saw you've been trying to get hold of me."

"Nothing to worry about," Ellie said, so of course Mabel started to worry. "I'm actually calling on behalf of someone else. Sam."

"You what? You don't even like him," Mabel said forcefully, dropping onto the stool in front of the kitchen's small island.

"I didn't. But."

"But?"

"But, I changed my mind. He was at Temple Sinai all day today. Jonah talked to him after the holiday ended, and—"

"He's still in town? I thought he would've left by now."

"He's definitely here."

Exhilaration had no business flooding her chest, yet there it was. "And?"

"You need to hear it from him, but…he has my endorsement. Know that for now, okay? I'm convinced, and that's why I'm reaching out to ask you to talk to him. I know you blocked him, and he says he didn't want to turn up on your doorstep uninvited, so I'm voluntarily serving as the intermediary. Can he just call you? I'll give him my phone if you don't want to unblock his number."

"Give him your…is he there with you right now?"

"He is. We're at the synagogue."

Mabel closed her eyes, tried to still her racing heart. "I'll unblock him. Give me a minute, and then he can call."

"You know I wouldn't do this if I thought it would make anything worse, right? Or if I had even the slightest doubt about whether it was in your best interest?"

"I trust you, Els. Hopefully I'll thank you, too."

"You might. I'll let you go. Speak soon."

Ellie hung up, and Mabel opened her contacts. She found Sam's number, tapped the three vertical dots to the right of it, and paused, her finger hovering over the unblock option.

She took a deep breath. Reminded herself she was strong, and valuable, and worthy. And with the faintest movement of her fingertip, let Sam back into her life.

Her phone rang almost immediately.

She stared at his name on the caller ID, her heart in her throat, not at all certain what the ideal outcome would be in this situation. She tapped the screen to answer.

"Mabel?" He was slightly breathless, like he was in motion, and she could hear the wind whipping around him, yet hearing those two syllables in his smooth, deep voice still sent a delicious shudder down her spine.

"What is this, Sam?"

"An act of sheer desperation? An attempt at a grand gesture by a lovesick fool? The last scene in a movie, when the dumb, undeserving guy turns up at the beautiful girl's house and wins her back despite all his flaws and mistakes. At least, that's what I'm going for."

Bewildered, she walked to the window and looked outside, but she saw nothing but the empty street.

"What are you talking about? And where are you?" she asked, holding the phone an inch from her ear as a siren shrieked on the other end.

"I'll show you."

She got a notification that he was trying to switch to a video chat. She accepted, past caring that her face was pale and puffy, squinting instead at Sam. He was barely visible in the darkness, but then he passed under a streetlight and the flash of his broad, bright smile had her heartbeat skittering.

"Can you see what I'm doing? I'm—oops, sorry." He almost collided with a jogger.

She sighed, but she wasn't nearly as exasperated as she sounded. She was curious, excited, and dangerously hopeful.

But he didn't need to know that.

"What *are* you doing?"

"I'm walking to you. I'm walking to your house. See?" He held up the phone and her screen filled with a blur of sidewalk and taillights and the intermittent, neon glow of shopfronts.

"I see. And I'm switching us back to audio-only so the whole world doesn't have to hear our conversation." She deliberately made her tone grumpy and impatient, but her heart had been replaced by a hummingbird, beating its wings into a blur in her chest.

She knew exactly what he was doing, and she hoped to God she was right about why.

"Better?" he asked, the one-to-one line feeling hushed and intimate after the speakerphone.

"Yes. Now would you like to tell me what the hell is going on?"

"I spent all day at Temple Sinai, thinking about the mistakes I've made, the regrets I have about our relationship. Leaving you in New York was stupid and reckless. Leaving you twelve years ago was even worse. But you said the love of your life would walk straight toward you, so that's exactly what I'm doing. Call it atonement, or symbolic, or just putting in the work—I love you, Mabel, and I want to prove it to you. This is the first step."

She closed her eyes, pressing her palm at the base of her neck in an attempt to keep all the oxygen from rushing out of her lungs.

It didn't work. The space between her ribs emptied, flattened, and then reinflated with a sudden rush that made her vision reel.

He loved her. And he was headed this way.

"From Temple Sinai," she murmured, and then frowned. "That's, like, three miles. Your leg—"

"Is much better, thanks to you. My whole life is… But we can talk when I get there. Is that okay? You're willing to see me?"

Willing? More like dying to see him.

"Yes," she said primly.

"Thank you. You won't regret it. I promise."

He hung up, and Mabel pressed the phone against her sternum.

He loved her.

He *loved* her.

She walked back to the front room and dropped onto the couch. He loved her—but did she still love him? More importantly, should she?

Walking three miles on a stiff leg took Sam over an hour, and gave Mabel plenty of time to process this unexpected twist in the ongoing plot of their relationship. Once the initial, dizzying combination of shock and exhilaration subsided, she forced herself to sit down and parse through her feelings rationally. She measured the lingering bitterness and hurt, compared it to her undiluted desire and affection for him, and did the emotional math as objectively as she could.

By the time she heard his footsteps on the stairs, she'd decided to give him one last chance.

She opened the door and gazed all the way up at him. He looked exhausted and anxious and desperate, but when he smiled, it was the most beautiful sight she'd ever seen.

"Sit down before you collapse." She motioned him toward the sofa but he stayed in the doorway, his expression intent.

"I love you, Mabel. Let me start there. I love you, and I don't want to lose you again. I came to Orchard Hill thinking this place made me who I am, imagining it could get me back to my best self—but it was never this town, or its people. It was you. It was always you. Everything good I've ever done is thanks to you, Mabel, and who you taught me to be."

She was frozen, unable to think, barely able to breathe. She could do nothing but stare at him, waiting to wake up.

Then the past roared up in her memory, a wave that crashed over her, deafening, choking, until she managed on a sob, "How can I believe you? How do I know you won't leave me again?"

He murmured her name, his forehead creasing in concern, and then he pulled out his phone, tapped the screen, and passed it over.

She blinked at it through welling tears, catching only a few words, passing the phone back more confused than when she'd taken it. "Helsinki? Is this your ticket? I don't know what I'm looking at."

"It's *your* ticket, if you want it. Fully flexible. Come for a week, see if you like it. Take a sabbatical and stay for three months. Or I'll quit my job and live here, or I can find something else in DC and you can move out there—whatever you want."

"You can't quit your job," she said automatically—and then the full force of what he was offering struck her like a bowling ball.

"I'll do whatever I have to—whatever you need me to do. I'm never leaving you again."

Her tears came freely now, the rest of her life rolling out in front of her, bigger and brighter than ever before. "I love you, too, Sam. I want us to be together. That's all I've ever wanted."

"Come with me," he urged, taking her hands in both of his. "Let's get out of this place that won't let us forget who we were, put some distance between that old story and the new one we're going to write. Not forever, but for a little while. Long enough to give ourselves a fresh start—a second chance."

"Third chance," she corrected, finally finding her smile.

"Details," he replied, his grin turning into a secretive, intimate smile. Then he tugged her into his arms, cradling her head against his chest.

She closed her eyes, letting him take her weight, letting him have it all—her heart, her hope, her forgiveness, her future.

"I love you, Sam," she whispered.

His grip tightened. "I'm sorry I ever let anything get between us. Losing you is the greatest regret of my life. It won't happen again."

She leaned back, pressed her palm to his cheek. "I believe you. And I want to run away with you. The hospital is expanding the midwifery program. I did what I set out to do, and although I'll miss it, it'll grow and thrive with or without me. How soon can we leave?"

"Day after tomorrow?"

"Let's go." She beamed up at him, this man who'd known her so long and so well.

"First things first," he told her, and then lowered his

mouth to hers.

Mabel lost herself to his kiss, mentally loosened her fists and let everything go—her mom, his dad, her absent father, his intruding mother, the decades of judgmental glances and muttered comments, and most importantly, that sweltering day in August when he'd walked away. All that was gone, and he was here, real, warm, solid beneath her hands, against her mouth.

Their love was insistent, defiant, more durable than she'd ever imagined, and now it would finally bind them together as it was meant to. Simply, easily, and without interference.

She loved Sam beyond reason. She trusted him beyond measure. She was ready to follow him around the world.

No, not follow. Walk hand in hand, side by side. Together and in love, as they were always meant to be.

Epilogue

"Hey, I just got signal. Oh, crap."

"Everything okay?" Mabel finished unpacking the overnight bag she'd brought for their long weekend trip to Lapland, then crossed the snug, secluded, treehouse-style cabin they'd rented to where Sam stood by a wall made entirely of glass.

"My brother's business is going belly-up. Sounds bad—really bad. He needs somewhere to stay, but I'll have to let him know I sublet the apartment in DC."

Sam started typing and she slid her hands on his shoulders, squeezing lightly.

"Zach could stay at my place in Orchard Hill if he's desperate. I'm still paying cranky old Mrs. Berger to store my stuff there, but it's such a tiny amount, I wouldn't expect him to cover it."

"I'll ask him."

Sam leaned forward, propping his elbows on his knees, and she drifted back to the little coffee station. She'd already wedged the bottle of champagne they'd brought into the minifridge underneath, and now she took time to examine the variety of coffee pods stacked in a tidy pyramid.

"Dark roast, French vanilla, ooh, maple," she murmured. She held up one of the pods as she turned to him. "Look, they've got maple-flavored—Sam?"

He was frowning at his phone, holding it at arm's length as if it might explode.

"More bad news?"

"Not exactly. Have you heard from your mom in the last couple of days?"

"Now that you mention it, I haven't. Why?"

"Because she's in New York. With my dad."

She dropped the pod, bolted across the room, and snatched the phone from his hand.

Sure enough, there they were, grinning in a badly taken selfie in front of the Christmas tree in Rockefeller Center.

"The last time we spoke she spent ten minutes complaining about her broken microwave, yet apparently forgot to mention this small detail," she remarked, handing him his phone.

"I'm glad they're happy. We are." He grabbed her around the waist, pulling her off balance and tugging her into his lap.

They were, too. The last two months had been a whirlwind in the very best sense. Whatever lingering remorse or wistfulness she had about leaving the program she'd built from scratch back in St. Louis vanished the minute she landed in Finland. She'd never had so much free time to simply relax and explore, and although she couldn't practice midwifery in Finland, she quickly made some professional connections and found opportunities to shadow and volunteer. The Finnish midwife-centered model of healthcare was an eye-opener, and even if she couldn't care for patients directly, she was learning a ton.

Sam grumbled about his pedestrian assignment, but this was her first trip to Europe, and every day felt like the adventure of a lifetime.

Meanwhile every night was better than the one before.

Sometimes it felt like they'd never been apart, she thought as Sam cupped her chin and brought her mouth to his. And sometimes they had so much to discover about each other, she wasn't sure a lifetime would be long enough.

That's what they had, though—a lifetime. She knew, without a doubt, that Sam wasn't going anywhere—and neither was she.

"When do we have to start watching for the northern lights? Because I have something I'd like to do first." He smiled up at her, his hand sliding suggestively over her butt.

"An hour or so. Is that enough time?"

"No, but I'll take what I can get."

She shrieked as he scooped her up and flung her over his shoulder, crossed the small room to the bed, and dropped her onto it. Then he crawled on top of her on all fours, kissing a line across her collarbone and up her neck.

"I had another email I want to talk to you about," he

murmured against her jaw.

"I see. Thought you'd get me in the right mood first, huh?"

"Maybe. It's about my next assignment."

Anxiety tightened her chest. She knew there would come a time when his job would separate them, when he'd go somewhere she couldn't follow, and she'd have to figure out where and how to wait for him to come home.

She just hadn't thought it would be so soon.

"It's a refugee camp in Kenya," he continued. "It's big, and pretty well established, so it's a short posting—ten weeks to do some operations assessments and troubleshooting. Thing is…"

Mabel held her breath, bracing herself for the worst.

"They have a lot of families there, and a lot of pregnant women. They could really use a midwife." He grinned. "Interested?"

She gaped at him. "Are you serious?"

He nodded, and she flung her arms around his neck, pulling him down so she could kiss him—hard.

"I love you, Sam. You know that, right?"

"I do. I love you, too—more than you'll ever know." His smile broadened. "We're going to have so much fun."

"I can't wait." She beamed.

Sam picked up where he left off, his mouth moving south this time, from behind her ear all the way down toward her breasts. She threaded her fingers through his hair and closed her eyes, sinking into the pure bliss of his touch.

One day they'd return to Orchard Hill. Maybe when they were ready to start a family, or if they tired of the nomadic life and wanted to settle down, or because something about that community called them back. The past would be forgotten, and they would start over there, a second chance at happiness.

In the meantime they were exactly where they belonged.

Together.

The End

Want more? Check out Eve and Saul's story in *Two Nights to Forever*!

Join Tule Publishing's newsletter for more great reads and weekly deals!

If you enjoyed *Coming Home to You*,
you'll love the next book in…

The Orchard Hill series

Book 1: *Shine a Light*

Book 2: *Two Nights to Forever*

Book 3: *Coming Home to You*

Book 4: *Home for Hanukkah*
Coming in December 2022

Available now at your favorite online retailer!

More books by Rebecca Crowley

The London Phoenix series

Book 1: *Insider*

Book 2: *Undercover*

Book 3: *Off the Record*

Available now at your favorite online retailer!

About the Author

Rebecca Crowley inherited her love of romance from her mom, who taught her to at least partially judge a book by the steaminess of its cover. She writes contemporary romance with smart heroines and swoon-worthy heroes, and never tires of the happily-ever-after. Having pulled up her Kansas roots to live in New York City, London and Johannesburg, Rebecca currently resides in Houston.

Thank you for reading

Coming Home to You

If you enjoyed this book, you can find more from all our great authors at TulePublishing.com, or from your favorite online retailer.

Made in the USA
Middletown, DE
17 December 2022